TIME PRESENT

BOOK 2

JAN C. SCHINDLER

What might have been and what has been
Point to one end, which is always present.

-T.S. Eliot, <u>Burnt Norton</u>

CONTENTS

CHAPTER 1
HARRY BEING HARRY

There are moments when I despair over my fate, but there is nothing I can do. I have to accept it. I try not to think about it, but it is hard sometimes. There is no one I can talk to that really understands. Minnie was the only one, and she was gone. I treasured being able to talk with her. She understood. I always knew she was smart. Harry and Ian are sympathetic, but they can't understand what I'm feeling inside. I dial down the emotions, sometimes adding a little mood enhancer. But the fact remains: I miss my life, my family, most of all my Minnie. And there is nothing, nothing I can do about it. I do still have my mind and all my memories. My outlook on this time, these strange people with their strange notions and strange planets, helps me realize I am still human. Harry and I have been on Earth for close to seven years now. Maybe it is time to venture out into the universe. Maybe staying here is keeping me melancholy. Earth is doing well.

Thor left after staying about six months with me. One day, he just up and left. Tulla had put a small tracker on him, and we watched him head back to the Appalachian

Mountains. He was healthy. He needed to be back in the wild, taking care of himself. After a month, we turned the tracker off. We had to let him be.

Harry went to help in the Ukarish conflict. They were allies of the Ca'Keenies, but were not members of the Alliance. The Ukarish were an evolutionary offshoot of the Ca'Keenies, having four arms and two legs. Their planet was located just out of RA proper, close to the Ca'Keenies' homeworld. They traded with them and other RA members in that sector. They had petitioned the RA central government for membership right before this latest conflict started. The Da'RiRaaans had attacked an Ukarish merchant ship.

The RiRas were in a system located further out of RA proper. They claimed the Ukarish home planet belonged to them. About 1500 years ago, there was a small settlement of RiRas on the planet. The settlers had renounced their citizenship and founded a small settlement. Soon after, a group of Ukarish settled on the other side of the planet. They had a successful business trading with others, including the rebel RiRas. An epidemic broke out in the RiRa settlement at some point. The Ukarish sent medicines, but the infection decimated the RiRas. It turned out to be a virus that the Ukarish were immune to, but the RiRas were not. The RiRa that survived returned to their home planet. Several months later, the Ukarish sent notification to RiRa and other nearby planets that they laid claim to the planet and system for the Ukarish. (There were two rocky planets and a gas giant in the system.) There were no objections from the RiRa initially. Eventually, the second planet was settled by the Ukarish and a small contingent of Ca'Keenies.

However, with a Da'RiRaaan regime change, there was a sudden interest in the system. There had been talks off and on for decades. The Ca'Keenies often brokered the talks, but lately the RiRa claimed they were biased against them. The Ca'Keenies and Ukarish repeatedly reminded the RiRas that the virus was still active on both planets. They couldn't understand why they suddenly were interested in the Ukarish system. Unless they had found a cure for the virus, they could not populate the planet.

The reason was simple and timeless: the Da'RiRaaans were expanding their empire in all directions. There were skirmishes throughout the decade, with the Da'RiRaaans attacking merchant ships trading with the Ukarish. RA sent an Alpha representative to try to negotiate with the RiRas. After twenty-eight years of peace, hostilities broke out again.

The Ca'Keenies sent out a general distress call for any kind of help. Harry and two other Ships responded. The Da'RiRaaans had superior weaponry and more fighters, but the Ships, hopefully, would turn the tide for the Ukarish. The RA sent three of their frigates to help. At the same time, Alpha sent out messages asking the Da'RiRaaans to come to the negotiation table. The RiRa answered with bombing one city on the planet. Several Ukarish fighters began harassing the RiRa ships, firing on them with low-yield weapons and zooming off into deep space. They would loop back, firing on them again. After several runs, the enemy ships followed, drawing them into deep space and away from any systems. The RA frigates attacked the RiRa ships, inflicting damage on them. *Torgun* destroyed one of the enemy cruisers. Unfortunately, more Da'RiRaaan ships arrived, materializing from alt.space and joined the battle.

Harry got notice that more RA ships were on the way. He chased one of the larger RiRa frigates. He noticed they were still in common space. He wanted to surprise them by going into alt.space and then popping back on top of them in common space. Harry, in his zealousness, winked into a neutron bomblet field the frigate had dispersed moments before. It destroyed him. One ship, the *Torgun*, contacted Harry to see if he was okay. The *Harry Houdini* was gone but his core unit, or his mind, was intact, drifting in space. He asked *Torgun* to send a message asking for me to come get him. After he made sure Harry was okay and I was en route, *Torgun* joined the battle several million kilometers away.

I WAS ENJOYING my visit to Venus 5. The LGM had terraformed a planet in the outer reaches of the Milky Way. It was a small system of four rocky planets, the middle one being Venus 5. It had mostly trees, but there were clearings and trails throughout the planet. There were several large bodies of water. They had trees from various planets and while most of them stayed as a monoculture, the LGM were experimenting with a mixture of trees in different groves. They had tiny houses scattered throughout the planet. The Ships had provided three weather satellites for them. It was pleasant sitting under the trees as their branches swayed in the gentle wind. I kept hearing what sounded like whispers that ebbed and flowed as the branches moved. I asked the LGM about this. There are some trees that can in fact "talk" to each other, but it is rare that they talk to anyone else. Those trees came from the LGM's home planet in that other universe. The LGM tried to communicate with them, but with no luck. I wondered if it was because the LGM used binary code to communicate with each other that made it hard for the trees to communicate with them. They weren't sure, but they had had no luck. I guess the trees just wanted to keep to themselves. The LGM were surprised I could hear them murmuring. They usually communicated in frequencies too high for human ears. I reminded Merrimun that I wasn't technically a human anymore. Perhaps my enhanced android hearing made the difference. I had talked to the trees, saying hello when I first arrived. I told Lorrimun, another LGM, that some humans had thought talking to plants helped them. He replied plaintively that they did talk to the trees. I suggested with a smile that they try English.

I learned that some LGM had created deserts on part of their Venus planets. They were unfamiliar with desert flora, but could take a just a few cells from cacti, succulents and other plants and grow them. They experimented with various elements, water and heat being the main ones to see what the optimum environment would be.

It was during a pleasant mid-day meal with Merrimun and Lorrimun that I received the message about Harry. I finished my lunch and thanked them for a wonderful visit. It pleased them I had taken an interest in their work and invited me to come back anytime. Harry had severed our connection when he went to fight. We usually stay open to each other, but I had no desire to know the blow-by-blow details of the fighting. We agreed before he left, we would communicate through the tachyon communicator.

I transported up to my ship. The M-droids had given me their latest small frigate. It was larger than a fighter, but not by much. It was a shiny silver ovoid shape with a bulge on either side about midway down from the tapered front. There was a control/observation deck slit of a window on its front. On either side of the bulge were shimmy guns, capable of firing nuclear bullets, lasers, photon torpedoes, you name it. I could change the method of destruction with a flip of a switch. The shimmy helped disperse the projectiles rapidly and in an even spread. At the front of the vessel in the control room was a dazzling array of switches, knobs, readouts, and LED numbers. It had a dedicated AI for flying and weapon operations. I could override it, but I let it handle the whole thing. It reminded me of the Ships of the Andromeda Galaxy, but much smaller. I wondered if the M-droids were paying tribute to the Ships.

The M-droids wanted me to test fly it, to see how the AI handled itself. I wondered if these AI were sentient, separate beings. Harry said they were, sort of, but in a limited capacity. They had specific functions, and that was it. They could carry on a conversation as long as it was superficial.

I always forget how vast space is and the gigantic battles that have been fought within them. Some wars involved an entire galaxy, like the Organic Wars. I checked my messages soon after takeoff. I noted I had received a garbled message from Harry saying he was in the middle of a battle with the Da'RiRaaans. Things were not going well even though the Ukarish were fighting bravely. Outgunned and outmaneuvered, and yet they inflicted damage to the Da'RiRaaans. The AI did not convey this message to me. It should have notified me immediately. The message was eighteen hours old. When I asked the AI about this, it couldn't give me a straight answer. Great! Something for the M-droids to look at later.

I knew I shouldn't have left him to go help with the war. The best source for additional help with the war was from the M-droids. They could manufacture just about anything one would need. I jokingly asked once if they could make a smaller washing machine with no water. Several hours later, a machine showed up at the gulf house. It used sonic vibrations to get rid of the dirt and various solutions to kill all microbes. The solutions evaporated after several minutes, leaving a subtle lemony fragrance. 21-5 sent a message with it, hoping I liked it. He said they were trying to come up with a method of transporting the dirt off the fabrics but hadn't had luck with nare blasted with cleaning solutions and water. The grey water is recycled back into the system, the chemicals neutralized. Many just recycle the clothes and then pick out new ones to wear using refigure machines to make them. There is a menu of over a hundred thousand styles from different cultures.

I entered ordinary space near the solar system and headed to Mars while I relayed Harry's situation to the other Ships.

I contacted 21-5 as I entered Mars's orbit and informed him of the grim situation. The M-droids had manufactured fifteen frigates and twenty-three starfighters along with various weaponry. The starfighters all had the newest upgrade. Their only function was war. The newest addition to the list of weaponry was the shimmy gun. There were larger sizes for ships, while there were smaller versions that were handheld. The smaller guns needed two people: one to shimmy and one to help hold the gun.

I told 21-5 about the communication kerfuffle. He found the glitch but said it would take several hours to fix. 21-5 did a cursory check and didn't find any other problems. I had to get back to find Harry, so I didn't wait for the repair to the ship.

A large transport followed along with a small squadron of droid controlled starfighters. There were fourteen of them; the rest would follow, as they needed some software upgrades performed on them. They loaded the frigates onto the transport and off they went. They could perform the final preps for the frigates en route.

I winked in close to where there was debris from a recent Ship destruction and warned the M-droid fleet about potential traps. The RiRa were famous for setting traps. I began my slow search. The rest of the fleet continued to the front lines.

I started doing sensor sweeps of the area with no immediate luck. As I said, space is vast. The ships moved off quickly and slowly disappeared into the black void. I set my sensors to maximum and identified the location of the frontline battle. After several hours, I picked up the chirp of a distress call within the debris field. I had to maneuver around all the space junk. As I got closer, the chirp got louder until I came upon its source a few meters in front of me. It was a rectangle box about six feet long, 1 ½ feet thick, and three feet wide.

"Claire, the exact measurements are 193.04cm by 60.96cm by 127cm. I believe that is the object you are looking for?" The AI was precise, if nothing else.

"Yes, can we get it into the hold?"

"It is initiated. There is ample room for it." A tractor beam latched on to the dark shape and brought it into the ship.

"I'm heading down there now."

The frigate was compact, but easy to move around in. I made my way to the hold near the back of the ship. There, in the middle of the deck, lay the object. There was a low hum coming from it.

"Oh, thank goodness for that." I gave out a sigh of relief. It had energy.

I walked over to it, entered the twenty-six-character code into the small recess panel. Its color changed to a deep blue. The hum faded.

An all-too-familiar voice asked, "Claire, is that you?"

"Yes, Harry, it's me. What the hell happened?"

"I got too close to a neutron bomblet. It's a good thing I encased my core in neutron spaghetti. Otherwise..."

"Yes, otherwise..." I sighed. "Where do you want to go?"

"M110. The Ships can help with my rebuild."

"You realize we are about a week away from there?"

"Yes."

I instructed the AI to head to M110. With that we entered alt.space; the M-ship effortlessly flew itself as I talked to Harry.

I started off telling him about the communication breakdown I had with the new ship. The rectangle box floated over to a terminal, projecting a thin green light to connect with it. Within a few minutes, Harry floated back and rested on the floor.

"An anomaly in the programming, but I think I got it fixed."

"21-5 told me it would take several hours to fix!"

"Well, yes, if you go layer by layer. I just went to its heart, so to speak. It seems this AI has a few extra programs. It wants you to give it a name."

"What? Okay, but this is kinda baffling. Is it miffed that it has no name?"

"Sort of. Just give it a name."

"Why me? The M-droids could have done that."

"It likes you."

"Oh, good grief! How about Mike? It sounds like a guy when it talks to me."

"Mike it is! Okay with you, Mike?" Harry asked.

"Yes, I like it a lot. Is Mike an Earth name, Claire?"

"Yes, it is."

"I doubly like it." He sounded smug.

"Back to more urgent matters. Harry, are you all here in this box?"

"You are looking at the Ship you call Harry. This 'box' contains all my functions, memories, thoughts, my mind map. It is all me."

"You had told me this a while ago, but I never really understood."

"Well, I exist throughout the ship, and it is a part of me, but not my essence."

"So, what happened?"

"I got careless. It was a pitched battle with the Da'Ri-Raaans. The Ukarish were inflicting some damage on four cruisers. I winked out, intending to wink back in behind a RiRa ship. I wanted the element of surprise, so I winked back in without scanning the area and the rest, you know."

"Ah, Harry, always something with you. I guess had you scanned, they would have known you were coming."

"Exactly! I take it the Ukarish won?"

"Yes, that battle, but there was still fighting in another sector. The M-droids have sent weapons and ships to help."

"Good! They need all the help they can get," Harry replied.

"So, will you... hold on. Mike, what is this I'm seeing on long-range sensors?" I asked.

"It appears there is a RiRa ship following us. They are slowly gaining on us."

"We can't deploy any weapons in alt.space," Harry said.

"Let's drop out of alt.space and use our new shimmy gun on them. Are you still reading only one ship, Mike?"

"Yes, dropping into common space now."

The ship entered ordinary space and immediately did a one-eighty. The RiRa ship dropped into common space right where Mike had expected it would be. He immediately let loose both shimmy guns. There was a slight vibration throughout the ship. The guns shredded the ship and an enormous explosion occurred, followed by a bright, expanding light. When the light dissipated, there was only a fine dust floating in the space where the ship had been.

"Impressive, Mike," Harry said. "Have to get me one of those."

"I'm sure they can arrange it," Mike replied.

I smiled. "Mike, there was a fine vibration throughout the ship. Is that normal?"

"Not sure. I have started a deep scan. The M-droids hadn't had time to test the guns properly. It may just be part of the gun function. I've sent out a status report on all my functions back to them, but it may take a while to reach them."

"Let's venture onwards to M110 and get Harry fixed. Any other ships pursuing us, Mike?"

"No, I'm keeping my long-range sensors on, so we should have plenty of notice if one should find us."

I sat down on the floor next to Harry in the cargo hold. Mike had the ship under control and was making good time in alt.space. I looked at the deep blue rectangular black box that was Harry. I placed a hand on him. The surface was quite smooth and cool to the touch. I could feel a slight, fine vibration.

Harry sighed. "I can feel your touch, my dear."

"I hoped so." I smiled. "So, what happened?"

"You know. The RiRas had the Ukarish on the run. Things were turning around when I blew myself up. The additional help from Mars should turn the war around. I am worried, though, as they are fighting close to the Ukarish homeworld."

"I think *Torgun* and *AS4966*, along with the M-droid

help, should keep them at bay. We need to get you fixed," I said.

"Yes. Maybe I'll change my appearance. I haven't been female in a long time. I was quite fetching." He chuckled.

"You can be anything you want, but I am used to you as a male, though. And would you change your name? Maybe to Harriet?" I replied with a slight smirk.

"Harriet? Sounds like I belong on a farm! No, I'll keep the look I had. I'm rather fond of it. I'm thinking of a light bluish cast to my skin instead of the yellow. What do you think?"

"Similar to what you look like now as a box? It looks like where I touched you, the blue was more pronounced."

"Yes, it is a reaction to you, my dear."

"I miss you. I want to hold you."

"As I do you. Hey! I could be female, and you could be male. That might provide some interesting experiences."

"Um, no. I'm happy with who/what I am."

"I understand. It's hard to change identities when that is what you are comfortable with. For me, my identity is located inside my mind map. External appearances don't matter. I've been many beings. It helps inform me, but is not essential to me."

"Yeah, one of my human hang-ups. Even after all this time as an android, I still think of myself as a human of the female variety. Like I said, though, if you want to be some-one/thing else, feel free."

"How about a Ca'Keenie?" I could hear the teasing mirth in his voice.

"Go for it!"

"Ha! No. I was one once. Never could get used to all those extra appendages. I could be a Bruthorian. Stark white with a pronounced greyish tint in areas, three eyes."

"They were rather startling. Very reserved."

"Yeah, I guess I'll stick with my light blue tint," Harry said wistfully.

"Sounds good to me."

"Seriously, though, you want to be the guy for a while?"

"Harry! Let's keep things as they were! It's just easier that way."

"Okay, my dear."

CHAPTER 2
NECESSARY DESTRUCTION

The Ships had scaffolding and large cranes set up in space to work on reconstructing Harry. They had a shipyard orbiting a brown dwarf with two small rocky planets. The planets provided some elements necessary for the construction. There were also non-sentient robotic ships that wandered the satellite galaxy collecting the various particles, atoms, molecules, and complex matter that were used in the rebuild. If a special material or energy was needed, these ships would venture beyond M110 to find it. Ship *192* handled their programing and upkeep. He had been involved in the Organic Wars and was happy to have the essential but mundane task.

They quickly made the framework for the *Harry Houdini*. They added neutron spaghetti to the frame per Harry's instructions. I watched with growing fascination as the ship came together. The hull was reinforced, along with an upgraded shield for the various EM radiations. Supposedly, the Vox had developed a potent gamma ray, but there was no evidence of it so far. There were several upgrades to engines and forcefields. The Ships took an interest in the shimmy gun and incorporated it into the rebuild. Harry could now help in the rebuild as they had placed his core into the Ship. They heavily protected the core, along with the energies used with additional shields. Harry recreated his avatar. There seemed to be a network of unique fibers coursing through the entire length and breadth of the Ship structure. Those same fibers were also in our avatar bodies. They are not organic in the sense of blood vessels and nerves, but seem to have a similar function. When I asked Harry about them, he said they were specially made and would not elaborate. I didn't push. There are still a few files not open to me. The Ships guard the information as to what and how they were created. Both he and I stayed on Mike for the duration of the refit. The Ships added some upgrades to Mike as well. *3.14159*, or Pi, oversaw the construction of the Houdini.

"I am amazed how quickly the rebuild of the Houdini is going," I said.

"We've had quite a lot of time to perfect the procedures. The basic construction starts out the same for all Ships. It is the details that can take time. For example, using the neutron spaghetti slows thing up as they have to find enough of it," Harry replied.

"Are there any new Ships being born?"

"Funny you should ask that. Pi mentioned there is talk about just that. Some Ships feel we should replenish our population. All of us originals were birthed a long time ago. We have lost a few through various mishaps and wars, but I think we still have plenty of us to go around."

"So, how many are you? Or is that a closely guarded secret?"

"We don't go around bragging, but our numbers are in the thousands spread out mostly among the three galaxies: Milky Way, Andromeda and Triangulum. Some have ventured beyond, as you know. And some are sprinkled throughout the local Group."

"So, the new ships, the babies, if you will, would be just that, your babies."

"True, only we birth them differently." Harry smiled. "I don't know why some are considering it. It takes massive quantities of matter and energy to start from scratch. Pi handles the total construction and repair of Ships and he is not too happy with the idea."

"What is their reasoning for it?"

"Ha, that's a good question."

It was into the third week that *Caddis* arrived. He got back to M110 as quickly as he could, even if it meant harming himself. He ran his engines over 125% and almost depleted all his energy. The engines were overheating and running ragged. His weaponry was offline and virtually non-existent. He needed some much-needed repairs. *Caddis* had disturbing news about the microbots.

Harry, by this time, had finished his rebuild. The shimmy guns were one of the last upgrades. Pi could manufacture them from studying the two on Mike. Harry had four. There were still system checks and finessing of weapons and shields, but the overall reconstruction of the *Harry Houdini* was finished.

"At first, the microbots seemed to ignore us, so we gathered a good bit of information about their creators," *Caddis* said. "There was an abandoned research station in the outer reaches of the system where we could tap into the memory banks. An abandoned orbital station wobbled around another planet. They called themselves Maratheusians or Maras. Their home planet was called Maratheu. They named the planets after their deities; Maratheu was the supreme goddess, and her consort was Marathane, another planet in their system. There were two moons circling Maratheu, named after her two children Tatatheu and Blenthane. They were an ancient civilization. They had advanced capabilities for traveling great distances, like winking, but it used less energy. Engines were smaller but very efficient in their ships; they did not use Hawking radiation. I've given that information to Pi to see if we can use it in our upgrades.

"They began creating microbots to venture farther out into the universe. Their system is not in any galaxy, rather isolated on the way to Andromeda IV. They originally wanted to use the microbots as scouts or ambassadors. The Maratheusians felt this would save them time and resources to eliminate primitive civilizations or unoccupied planets. They were in the early stages of this exploration. Apparently, some of these scout microbots got as far as the Milky Way and sent info back about it.

"They also used the 'bots to help in their daily living and culture, everything from helping with food production to medicine to space flight to building orbitals and stations. The Maras kept tinkering with their code and altering key parts of the programming. It looked like the programming having to do with harmful microbes was the source of the microbots' aggression. What is disturbing is that it seems the microbots identified with the pathogen or microbes' programs and altered their own programming. The Maras were not aware of this until it was too late. The microbots became self-aware. For all their advanced knowledge and technology, the organics created tiny monsters.

"It wasn't until we orbited Maratheu that the 'bots took noticed of us. *Bormador* and Energy sent droids down to the surface. I hung back, monitoring the microbots. There were ruins of several cities on the planet. I have video of them right until the 'bots attacked the Ships. They left me alone and focused on the other two ships. There must have been a contingent of them on the planet, for they came out of nowhere and swarmed over the droids. It happened so fast that by the time *Bormador* and Energy put up their defensive shields, the microbots were already trying to access their systems. The only thing the Ships could do was to destroy themselves and so they did. They sent their cores to me, and I immediately put them into stasis. I also put a force-fifteen shield around them. I scanned them for any evidence of 'bots and found none. All this while running my engines above 100%. I didn't want to take any chances, so I sent two antimatter torpedoes into their sun and blew the whole system up. Small bits of matter and erratic strains of stray energy were all that was left of them."

"Do you think that was necessary, *Caddis*? That was a rather severe reaction," Pi asked.

"If they had accessed Ship systems before I blew them up, then they would know how to defeat us," *Caddis* replied. "So, it wasn't a severe reaction, but a matter of existence. Just imagine if they had access to *Bormador* and Energy."

"Well, this has to go before the Ten. I'm sure they are probably aware of it," Pi said.

"I just got a message from AS 6. They are on their way here," *Endtimes* said.

"This should be interesting," Harry said, "I can't recall

them ever getting together for a transgression. Too busy navel gazing."

"Harry, do you really think they would annihilate *Caddis*?" I asked.

"I don't see how they could. He acted to protect all the Ships. If it comes to that, I'll become a Renegade, and tell them to go suck on a pulsar," Harry replied.

"It won't come to that, Harry," *Caddis* said. "I'll probably be exiled for a few years from M110.

"Anyway, as best as I can tell, the Maras were a rather advanced civilization. Had interstellar travel and some interesting energy sources. Pi gave that info over to the Ships to see if it is anything we could use. Cities, though in ruin, were still imposing. They seemed well planned. We could access their cultural files. They had a fondness for music. The one thing we weren't able to access easily was the specs on the microbots. *Bormador* found the files, and it was at that point that the 'bots attacked them."

"He didn't transfer those files to you, did he?" Harry asked.

"He did, though he didn't get all of them, but I think we can figure out the gaps. Along with running myself ragged to get here, I looked over the files. Some interesting stuff. I sent those files with everything else to all the Ships."

"Let me guess," Harry mused, "sentience or consciousness was not part of the program."

"It appears that way, although there are those gaps..." *Caddis* replied.

"So, the 'bots killed the Maras, all of them?" I asked.

"Yes, so it seems," *Caddis* said.

"All because of a misinterpretation of some code. Rather sad," I replied.

Harry sent 21-5 all the info on the microbots. He did a

quick scan of the programming files and noticed it was similar to the Regional Alliance's nano technology. 21-5 thought he found where the Maras went wrong in the coding that allowed for sentience. He was in touch with Pi and relayed his initial impressions. The M-droids were working on improving the dome shields around the planets. I conveyed my thanks to 21-5. He was glad to hear his ships made the difference in the Ukarish war. They finally had the Da'RiRaaans on the run. Good for them!

I talked to Reedmer to catch up on all the news from his end. As usual, he was his gregarious self. He has enjoyed his new life in *Caddis*.

"I saw some wonderful phenomena on the way to Maratheu. It took us a while to get there, so *Caddis* would point out different things for me. We couldn't stop, but it was enough to see them. There were three black holes we passed. *Caddis* said they weren't big like the ones at the centers of galaxies, but he sucked up energy from them for fuel. That was kind of scary. It looked like we were going to go into the hole at first. The Ships are really amazing! How are you doing, Claire? *Harry Houdini* back in action?" Reedmer asked.

"He is. He's analyzing the microbot info to see where things went wrong with them. We've talked a little about what we're going to do next."

"Those 'bots seemed rather benign at first. And then, they just swarmed over the droids on the planet like ants. The droids didn't have any time to react. Two droids fired their weapons, one even blew itself up but there were just too many of them. *Caddis* got the hell out of there. Both *Bormador* and Energy sent out destruct codes. *Caddis* knew there wasn't anything he could do."

"I don't understand that. The droids were on the planet

and the Ships orbiting the planet. How did the 'bots get access so fast?"

"*Caddis* was asking those same questions most of the way home. Not sure. There were open lines of communication with the ships. Maybe that way? I don't think they really know. Maybe Harry can find out," Reedmer replied. "Otherwise, how are you doing, Claire? Besides all this fanfare."

"I'm okay. I think spending time on Earth has helped me. It gently forced me to make peace with my situation. At least, it made me realize Earth is just in a new era, one without humans, and is doing just fine. It also gave me time to accept my new body. I still think of myself as human even though my body is not." I gave a short laugh. "Harry helped. He tends to offer his opinion on every little situation. I think he was driving the droids a little batty. He visited the M-droids a lot. We visited the LGM occasionally too, toured the moons of Saturn, stuff like that. It was nice, but even I started to feel restless. I have to give it to Harry. He never once tried to push me to go. He gave me as much time as I needed. I'm concerned about this meeting of the Ten, Reedmer. I hope it turns out favorable for *Caddis*."

"You and me both," Reedmer said. "First time I've heard of this, so I had to access some files. The Ten are the first Ships born."

"Yep, that is what Harry says, though he had some choice words about them. *They* decided they would be the leaders of the Ships. They created what Harry calls guidelines for Ships' behavior, but Ships do whatever they want, mostly. Harry said the use of weapons is a sticking point with the Ships. There is an unwritten rule that states that if all Ten find harm, then they could destroy *Caddis*," I replied.

"I tried to find out if they have ever destroyed any Ship and couldn't find any examples. At least, there's that."

"Surely they wouldn't do that. I mean, they would destroy ME too!" Reedmer paused. "The Ten have summoned me; it looks like they have arrived."

CHAPTER 3
SHIP JUSTICE

The Council of Ten met on *One*'s ship. In the conference room were chairs of various shapes and sizes arranged in a semi-circle for the avatars of the Ships. There was a long table for the ten avatars. They were mostly bipedal, although *Seven*'s avatar was a three-armed, three-legged Vargarian. The Vargarians lived in the upper-left quadrant near the edge of M31. They did not take part in the Organic Wars. The bipedal avatars had various colored skin and hair. The only exception was *Nine*. His avatar was a metal robot complete with blinking lights and a synthesized voice. Instead of legs, it rolled in on wheels. Claire turned to Harry and subvocalized, 'what's the deal with the 'bot?' Harry shrugged and replied that *Nine* was rather eccentric and loved to irritate the rest of the group.

They placed Reedmer's mind map in a special box and put it on a chair in front of the Ten. He related what had happened after they got to the Maratheu system. He explained the Ships did not want to confront the 'bots, only to understand their purpose. They wanted to engage with their creators but discovered instead the ruined planets.

"Was there a discussion about just leaving?" *Four* asked.

"Not that I remember," Reedmer said. "The consensus was to go to the major planet and meet the microbot creators. We were looking forward to discussing their science and culture with them. The Ships had traveled several weeks to get there. We did not consider turning around."

Reedmer relayed the information to the Ten, much like *Caddis* had to Pi and Harry. There was no room for hesitation because everything had happened so quickly. He also conveyed *Caddis*'s remorse at destroying the system, but felt it was the only thing to do. He had seen the destruction the microbots had caused for the Regional Alliance. *Caddis* knew they were an existential threat to Andromeda, M32, M110 and the Milky Way. Reedmer ended with praise for *Caddis*'s bravery in a very tense situation.

"So, Reedmer, it is your opinion that Ships' life is more important than an entire society of beings?" *Three* asked.

"Yes, absolutely, when those beings, as you call them, are hellbent on destroying you. Ships should use whatever is available to them to defend their existence. Was it excessive force? I don't think so. We found microbots throughout the Mara system, hence the system had to be destroyed."

"Thank you for your testimony, Reedmer. We shall hear from *Caddis* now."

Caddis walked to the center of the semicircle and took a seat next to the box that was Reedmer. His avatar was stunning. He looked like a Fluton, with red and blue feathers on his head and piercing emerald-green eyes. His skin was a bright blue. He was tall for a Fluton, about two meters. He wore a grey vest that showed his well-formed arm muscles and long, tight grey pants. Claire did a mental sigh. Harry looked at her with an amused look.

"*Caddis*, I think we understand the circumstances of the destruction. What we are interested in now is your thought processes as to the decision to destroy the system," *Ten* said.

"I'm not sure you do understand. Do you not have the memories I sent to you that showed the processes that led to the destruction? You should pay attention to the time-stamps. There were only milliseconds of time to make decisions," he replied with a raising of his voice. Harry subvocalized to *Caddis* to calm down. Getting angry didn't help, even though they were second-guessing his every move.

"Yes, we have scrutinized those memories and still do not understand why you hadn't considered any alternatives."

"Again, there was no time. I just saw two of my friends blown up by these entities that I did not consider sentient. Everything happened at once. The microbots swarmed. The droids battled them and were overwhelmed. Droids being overtaken by the infestation, and blowing themselves up in a last desperate attempt to stop them. Then *Bormador* and *Energy, Life Blood of the Universe*, were obliterated by their self-destruction, the ultimate sacrifice. I wasn't sure if they had self-destructed or if the microbots had overtaken them. There were attempts on myself by the 'bots trying to access my systems. I did what I thought was the only thing I could do. I spent my escape back to here, scrubbing my files, making sure not one 'bot got a toehold in me. I had both mind maps stored in my cargo hold with a force 15 shield around them. I held both in suspension and scanned continuously for the microbots."

"If I may, *Ten*," Harry interrupted, "I just received a communication and decree from the Regional Alliance. They were glad to hear we destroyed the microbots as they posed a threat to RA. They thank *Caddis* and the Ships for their sacrifice. All the twenty-four system members signed the degree. There are approximately thirty-seven trillion beings in the RA."

"Thank you for that, Harry," *Nine* said. "I think *Caddis* did the only thing he could do."

"*Caddis*, is there anything you wish to add?" *Ten* asked.

"No, you have my files, my memories, my thoughts," he replied.

"*Sumador*, I understand you wish to speak?" *Ten* asked.

"If I may. I spoke with my brother before he left. *Bormador* understood the risks involved with the microbots. He encountered them in the Milky Way, so he had a good sense of what they were. He hoped there wouldn't be any confrontation with them. *Bormador* wanted to meet their creators. I read the reports *Caddis* provided us and I am convinced that he did the only thing he could by destroying the Maratheu system. I don't think he had any other choice. If I may add, *Caddis* and my brother were friends, good friends. I only hope that my brother's mind map is still intact; that he and Energy can be rebuilt."

"I understand that Pi and *AS666* have looked at their mind maps and think that we can restore them, Suma. We will do all we can to have them rebuilt. The risk is that the 'bots could have infiltrated their cores. We are running tests and scans to determine that. It is a delicate process. Working with force fields is difficult too," *Five* offered.

"Thank you, *Five*. I appreciate that," Suma replied.

28

"We will confer with each other and let you know what we decide." With that, the ten avatars left the room.

Caddis was angry that he had to defend himself to them but respected the Ships' traditions, even if they hadn't used them for thousands of years. The Ten seldom interacted with other Ships. It was a source of contention that they did not help in the Organic Wars.

"Harry, what do they hope to gain by this?" *Caddis* asked.

"Hell, I was never much of a fan of theirs, especially after the Organic Wars. I don't think I can forgive them for that. Maybe, in a twisted way, they think this is atonement for their earlier non-involvement. I think, though, it is only going to solidify opposition to them. They spend most of their time in M32, anyway. They ought to just stay there and leave the rest of us alone."

Caddis replied, "Yes, we all know how you feel about them, Harry."

"Harry feels strongly about many things and the Ten are high on his list. I made the mistake of accessing a file of his called 'Ten'. Woah, boy! I learned what a dinkerdum was. Pretty vile beings, not too bright. He even offered to take me to their planet. No thanks!" I said with a laugh.

"Please understand, *Caddis*, I hold no ill will towards you," Suma said. "I only hope I'll see my brother again. I just get the feeling the Ten are holding back on something."

"That's just their 'mysterious' way. When I scanned *Bormador* and Energy's cores, there was energy, but it was weak. I tried to boost it, but they were slow to absorb it, especially Energy. I didn't want to do a full reboot. They needed to be checked first. I saw no evidence that the 'bots had infiltrated their maps, but I was in turmoil, trying to get away as fast as I could. Maybe something was over-looked. Pi will figure it out," *Caddis* said.

"I do plan to check with Pi," Suma said.

"Could there be internal damage the scans didn't pick up, *Caddis*?" I asked.

"Yes, there was a lot of high energy zapping around before and after I blew the whole thing up. They may have gotten a small dose of the antimatter as I trans-ported the boxes at the same time the explosions went off," *Caddis* said. "Harry, how did you survive your neutron bomblet?"

"Neutron spaghetti. I encased my core with it. You weren't in range to receive the upgrade message. I think most of the Ships are using it now," Harry replied.

"Send me the specs and I'll do it," *Caddis* said.

The Ten returned after several hours. They sat down at the table. The others sat in the semicircle with *Caddis* in the center. He integrated Reedmer into him once again. It seemed the Ten had dialed down all their emotions. Their faces were blank, devoid of any expression except for *Nine*. His metallic eyes focused on *Caddis,* and he nodded his head in reassurance.

One spoke: "It has been an overriding principle that Ships do no harm to other sentient beings. This came about because of the Organic Wars. The Ships may have to defend themselves, but massive slaughter is not acceptable. This happened in the Maratheu system. I do not think it was necessary to destroy the entire system. There are several of my fellow Ships who disagree with me. In the end, we came upon a compromise. *Caddis* is exiled from Andromeda for three hundred years."

One, *Three*, *Four*, *Eight* and *Ten* got up and left. *Two* let out a sigh of relief.

"Seems like there are some hard feelings, *Nine?*" Harry asked.

"Oh, they'll get over it. With the split down the middle, there was no chance of obliteration. Several of us wanted to forget the whole incident, but *One* wasn't having it. I haven't seen her worked up this much in a long time. I told her to dial it down or I would zap her." *Nine* laughed. "I have this little electrical charge I can generate in my claws. It is unpleasant but harmless."

"Are you going to stay as a robot, *Nine*? I know how you love exploring different personas and bodies," Harry asked.

"Probably not. I did it just to irritate *One*. She lacks a sense of humor. She made several veiled remarks about it. I just waved my arms like the robot in the original *Lost in Space*, and she told me I was ridiculous! Normally, the individual Tens are off by themselves either exploring a part of M31 or 32, or just cruising around with no real purpose. Ha! I just realized that the Ships that sided with me were the ones that do some exploring. Interesting. Anyway, Harry, some of the old Ships like *Twelve* and *Fifteen* have just wandered off entirely. *Sixteen*, *Seventeen* and *Twenty* left to explore the Triangulum Galaxy. That was about eight hundred years ago. We used to get updates initially from *Twenty* but after one hundred, thirty- six years those stopped."

"I'm impressed, *Nine*, that you know about *Lost in Space*," I said. Will I ever get used to the references to Earth from other beings? Earth's pop culture seems to have traveled far. I smiled to myself.

"Harry had shared all the information he gathered from Earth over the Earth centuries with all the Ships. The science fiction genre is fascinating. I've read all the books and seen the TV programs and movies. Don't like the 'superheroes genre' but a lot of it I truly like and enjoy. I was sad to hear about Iain Banks' death. He is a favorite of mine. I am sorry there won't be more scifi stories coming," *Nine* replied. "So, where to now, Harry? Want to hang around here?"

Harry laughed. He had no desire to stay. He was ready to head back to the Milky Way. *Caddis* headed to the Regional Alliance, where he would offer his help with whatever they might need. Harry thought it was an excellent decision. We said our goodbyes and winked to the outer reaches of the Milky Way. We entered alt.space to arrive at RA space in a few days.

CHAPTER 4
CLEE

I found Harry in a small observation lounge on the *Houdini*, staring out of the window, watching the smears of light go by. I tried accessing his superficial thoughts and found them closed off. He shifted his weight from one leg to another, bent leg, straight leg much like Polyclitus's Canon, the Doryphoros. He has a more Praxiteles body with shoulders I so much enjoy looking at. I smiled to myself.

"I can make my shoulders wider if you like, my dear." His back was towards me. I walked up behind him and wrapped my arms around his waist. I put my head against his back. The heartbeat sound was soft and regular. He put it there for me.

"No, you are perfect just the way you are," I said as I let go of his waist and stepped around to his side.

"Oh, no! Now I'm going to get a swell head." He laughed. He turned and kissed me lightly on the cheek.

"What are you thinking about that you had to shield from me?"

"I apologize. I wasn't even aware I had done that. When I think about things, I delve into arcane files and forget that I've locked those files. It's a security I added before you came aboard." He smiled and kissed the top of my head. He had made himself almost a foot taller than me.

"Harry, I understand. You told me at the beginning of this, um, endeavor that you would keep certain files locked to me until I got comfortable with my new body. I have gained some of your knowledge, ya know. But I'm still not interested in how the engines work and all that 'sciencey' stuff, especially the math!" I started laughing. He always got annoyed when I disparaged math.

He cut me that look that was part stern and part amusement. "I'm glad to see your love of math is *so* overwhelming!"

"I have access to some of the math. I hid it from you because I wasn't sure where it would lead me. There is a resistance in my psyche about it. It seems stripped of emotion. The artist in me wants some emotion, not just cold facts. I don't want the universe reduced to zeros and ones. I guess that is a strange way of putting it. Anyway, a penny for your thoughts, dear heart?" He sometimes got a dreamy look when he was lost in thought.

"I was thinking about tachyons," he replied. "Pi gave me a file of his research on them. He's trying to find an alternative safer energy source for winking out other than Hawking radiation."

"How would that even work? Aren't tachyons virtual particles? I mean, no one has seen any evidence of them in experiments, right?"

"Well, that was true until a few months ago. Pi figured out how to detect them and developed a way to collect and store them. He was using a lined container with several elements that don't interact with the tachyons. It was about a meter square. Efforts to make it bigger failed, so he's working on that. Maybe the container doesn't have to be all that big. I saw his calculations and am stymied by them. Yes, me! Don't give me your smarty pants look! He is also trying to gather more bits. Apparently, it is difficult to catch them. If it works, it'll really help with the winking. He's also looking at the info *Caddis* got from the Maratheusians. Maybe there's a clue in there. If anyone can figure it out, it is Pi."

"Can you use dark energy?"

"The problem with dark energy is that it doesn't seem to interact much with our universe. Pi tried to work out a way to use it. The prototype ship was small. He got it to work for about a minute and then it exploded! He had some damage to his systems, so he tried to find a safer way. I hope his new endeavor will be more successful.

"He improved communications with tachyons. It is only text and voice, no video, but it is faster than light. A much less time lag."

"I bet C would enjoy talking with him. He stayed on as energy czar and Ian is quite pleased with his work. I got a communique from Ian while I was transporting you to M110. It was several weeks old, but he gave me an update on what was going on in RA and Earth. Both were well. He listed the usual squabbles among members with all the petty gripes. I think it was his way of venting."

"He's still Prime?"

"Yes, although he was working with Deatine to have her step in. She had worked with him when he was First so, hopefully, she can take over for Ian as Prime soon, if not already. He'd much prefer to write and play music."

"The problem is that Ian is very good at being Prime

35

and the ministers know it. Deatine has big shoes to fill." Harry smiled at his use of the Earth idiom. "The few times I've met her, she impressed me, and I think she'll be a good Prime. It'll also be good for RA to have someone else besides a Kneff. New people, ideas. Politics!"

"I tried to stay out of politics. Earth politics was a slugfest, in my opinion. People being greedy. There was such a difference of opinion between it and the everyday reality. The politics are different here, but politics all the same."

"Yes, even us Ships have a version too, as you recently saw with *Caddis*. There has been some talk about abolishing the Ten's power and their outmoded sense of justice. There are some Ships, though, that think we should just keep things as they are."

"Could *Caddis* have just ignored their summons?"

"He could have, but then there are those factions that support the Ten. I'm not sure what they would have done except ignore him, maybe. But that is not the way of Ships. I think this happening showed the Ships the silliness of keeping this tradition alive. Anyway, I think *Caddis* can do good in the Milky Way."

"You know, I've never actually told Ian about our... um... involvement," I said. "I mean, I assumed he'd figure it out since I'm an android and you created my..." I stopped and looked at Harry. He had one eyebrow cocked up, lips pursed, and a devilish gleam in his eyes. "What? What did I say to provoke that look?"

"My dearest, you *do* know that Ian and I talk from time to time. He knows about us. He gave me a stern warning to always keep you safe as we go gallivanting across the universe. So, don't worry."

"Gallivanting? He said that?" Harry nodded. I laughed. "Yeah, and look who needed looking after. Ha!"

"Don't Ha me, young lady!" With that, Harry grabbed me and kissed me as I continued to giggle.

CADDIS SENT a message as they neared RA space. He and Reedmer flew on to Quozan. Reedmer was looking forward to seeing his homeworld. The Quozanants had a hero's welcome planned for *Caddis*: a week-long celebration with light festivals, parades, dance performances, music concerts, and official dinners.

Harry and I headed to Alpha, sending Ian and C messages of our soon-to-be arrival. We were all glad to hear of the hero's welcome for *Caddis*. We talked of trying to get back there, but I wanted to see my son and to spend time on Earth. C sent a message saying he had a surprise for us.

As we entered orbit, we received a welcome message from Deatine, the new Prime Minister of the RA. She was glad we were back and extended an invitation for us to visit her at the ministry's central office. She asked about having Earth join RA even though it was far away. It seemed Deatine wanted to incorporate some outer isolated systems into RA. It made sense, especially from a defensive position. I replied to her query about Earth by saying it sounded good, but I wanted to see the complete agreement before I considered it. She sent the files over with a hope to see us soon. It was a rather long document. I skimmed it and it seemed fine, but I wanted to study it in detail. I'd wait until we were on Earth to read it.

We transferred to a shuttle and landed at the smaller star port outside of the city. C was waiting for us as we disembarked. He had a big grin on his face. Iryna was with him, holding a child's hand. She looked about eight years old.

Harry and I looked at each other, surprised. We had been gone too long.

As we got close, the child, a little girl, broke from Iryna's hand, ran towards me calling "Geegee, Geegee". She wrapped her little arms around me. There were mostly Kneff features but with dark curly hair and startling ice-blue eyes. She was thin like a Fluton, and I mentally put two and two together.

"Mom, this is Claireena your granddaughter. We call her Clee. Iryna and I got married about a year after you and Harry left Earth. We've told her about you, showed her pictures, and let her listen to some of your vid messages. She has anxiously been awaiting your arrival. She couldn't say grandmother, so she settled on Geegee. Harry, good to see you. We knew of your demise and resurrection and we're glad you are okay," C said.

"All in a day's work. Claire rescued me, but that story can wait. What a lovely daughter you have. I bet she's smart like her mom and dad."

"I am," Clee giggled, "are you Harry?"

"Yes, Clee. I am a good friend of your Geegee." He smiled and effortlessly picked her up. She giggled and threw her arms around his neck. She whispered to him she liked him and knew he was really a big ship in the sky. Harry's eyebrows shot up and C explained that she over-heard himself and Iryna talking about Harry's recovery.

"We have a hover car so we can take you to the house. We are all living in the ancestral home, as we like to call it."

"I bet Ian's mom is thrilled about that!" I said, a bit sarcastically.

"Oh, you don't know. Sera is in a care home now. She

got an infection of some sort, and it affected her brain. She and some friends would take trips to 'primitive' planets just to visit and to start talks about trade with them. It was rather informal with Ian's mother thinking it would be of benefit to RA. Some pathogen apparently got by the bio-filters on their ship. Her two friends were also sick, but not as severely as her. One day she was fine and the next she was in a coma. It occurred about eight months ago; they are still trying to figure out what happened."

"I am sorry to hear. I did not know," I said, chagrined. "How is Ian with this? He must be upset."

We got into the car. Clee, myself, and Harry were in the back. C took off towards the house.

C continued: "Dad is okay. He and grandmother had a... um... complicated relationship. There have been investigations and reports about what went on. We isolated the three women until they found the pathogen was not contagious. Turns out on that planet, it is a rather common micro-organism. It appeared to have a unique makeup, and the filters didn't recognize it as a lifeform, much less a dangerous one. They are still researching it. Dad can tell you more about it."

"Well, I'm sorry to hear it, even though she wasn't the friendliest person. So, Deatine is Prime now. I bet your dad was happy about that! When did that happen?"

"Oh gosh, about two years now, maybe? Yes, he is quite happy! You are just in time to hear his new symphony. It debuts in one week. He has been rehearsing every day, three or four hours a day."

Iryna chimed in. "Tell her about Kannika, C."

Harry replied, "Oh dear, I had forgotten about her. She is your former partner's paramour, Claire."

"And I'm just now finding out about it?" I exclaimed.

"It's fairly recent, mom, and well, we weren't sure if it was a passing thing or not."

"Apparently, it's not," I replied.

"She sings, Geegee, in Opa Ian's music thing. She sounds pretty, but she's kinda strange," Clee said.

"Claireena! That is not polite!" her mother scolded.

"O, brother, is she staying at the house too?"

"No, but she is there a lot."

"What's this about singing in Ian's symphony?"

"There's a part where she sings an aria. He can tell you more."

We approached the house. C set the hover car down, and we all filed out. Ian was at the door. He looked happy and healthy. He gave me a big hug, slapped Harry on the back, and kissed his granddaughter. Clee promptly related what they had said in the car. Ian pretended to be shocked but started laughing at her reenactment of the conversation.

'This is new. He looks so relaxed,' I subvocalized to Harry.

'Yeah, I guess not being Prime does that. I'm happy to see it. That slap on my back was unexpected!' Harry said.

Bo greeted us as we entered. She gave me a hug and a nod to Harry.

"So, Ian, how is your aria coming along?" Harry asked.

"Cat's outta the bag, eh, Claire?" Ian said. "I was looking for a singer while I was writing the aria. I needed someone with a wide vocal range. She auditioned along with three other candidates and was the best. We became involved only recently. She will be here tomorrow. We are rehearsing her parts. I think it sounds great, but Kannika thinks she can sing better. You both can meet her then. She knows about you, Claire, but only in a general sense."

"I'm happy for you, Ian. You should know that!"

"I do. It's just I didn't know how you'd react. I mean..." Ian stammered.

I rolled my eyes at him. "It is not a problem. The bigger surprise is Clee. I am sorry I was not here for her birth."

"Yeah, you were too busy rescuing Harry!" Ian gave a short laugh.

"Geegee, tell me about space and your trips! I can show them the rooms they are staying in, Daddy. Harry, how is it possible you are a Ship?"

On and on she chattered as we walked down the hall to our rooms. She brought us to a spacious bedroom with an attached bathroom. There was another smaller room on the other side of the bath. It was a sitting room, or library. It had a large desk with a Knowledge terminal. There were two stuffed chairs facing a fireplace with a small sofa perpendicular to it. There were books on shelves opposite the fireplace. They were in various RA languages, including a few in English. I smiled; the *Odyssey* and *Iliad* were on the shelf. There was a mythology book that had all the ancient myths of Earth included in it.

I told Clee we were tired. She bid us *adieu* and skipped down the hall.

"Tired?" Harry chuckled. "We don't get tired unless we deplete our power source."

"It was the simplest excuse. I need to process a little that I am a grandmother, Harry. Were we gone *that* long?"

"Well, as usual, it depends on your frame of reference. She looks about 7-9 Earth years?" he replied.

"That seems about right. I know Kneffs mature differently from humans but..."

"She must be mostly Kneff though, Iryna must have

41

some Fluton in her. They mature even faster. The Earth genes seem to have manifested with the curly hair."

"Yes, humanity's contribution to the galactic gene pool. Ha! So, I guess we need to stay a little while for the premiere of Ian's new music, but I want to head to Earth after that. I got a message from Nimbo that things are good there. They saw Thor in the Appalachians. There was a den nearby with a female bobcat and two kits. He is doing well. The droids determined they were his!"

"I saw that! Did you see the communique from Pi?"

"I did, but just scanned it. Lots of energy talk. I saw where he mentioned C and said something about visiting Alpha?"

"Apparently, the Marathuesian files reaped benefits. All the technical jargon was about modifying some of the energy technology. He sent a detailed file to C. He may come here soon. Which is interesting because Pi usually doesn't venture beyond M110."

"What shall we do in the meantime?"

"Well, I can think of a few things." Harry had a rather devilish smile.

"Oh, you rake! You're always thinking about one thing." I started laughing.

He wrapped his arms around me and gave me a long, delicious kiss. From another part of the house, we could hear singing. We both smiled.

"Shall we retire to the boudoir, Madame?"

"Why, yes, sir, we should."

LATER, I got up and wandered around the house as Alpha's sun rose to create another day. Beta was setting as the sun rose.

The house was much like I remembered. The layout was the same. Not as many bedrooms, and the overall rooms seemed smaller. I liked that; no grandiose reception hall or large dining room. I heard clanging towards the kitchen and found Bo supervising two domestic robots.

"Bo, as usual, cooking up new and exotic dishes for the lowly organics."

She laughed and gave me a hug. I was glad to see her.

"No more chocolate chip cookies for you! Harry did a fantastic job on your android body. Have you adjusted to being in it?"

"Yes, I have, mostly. Although I crave cookies now and then! I can eat. It is just processed differently."

"Ahh, yes, the avatar body! Us lowly droids don't have that function. I am glad he saved your voice. Sounds like my Claire. Come, tell me what has been going on."

And so, I sat at the bar and related my past adventures as I had done when I first landed in this strange time and place. She had a good laugh over Harry's rescue. Bo recalled that had happened before. She remembered Ian being worried that Harry wouldn't return.

"Speaking of Ian, I thought I heard singing last night. Is she here?"

"She is. Kannika stays here most nights. Ian seems happy with her; that's all that matters. And don't feel guilty about your relationship. I think you and he were what you needed at that time. I could see you struggling with all the newness and strangeness of your situation. Harry is the better player. But I'm prejudiced towards us non-organics."

"I am glad for him as well. Clee made a comment that she is strange?" I asked.

"You'll see. Her music is all important to her. Clee interrupted her singing a few times. The first time Kannika just

43

froze, as in no motion, almost catatonic. One time she let out such a high-pitched screech it hurt Clee and Bortho's ears. Ian had a talk with Clee, and she went wailing to her father. C is a softy with his daughter. I think the earth expression is 'wrapped around your finger' Anyway, I don't think Kannika is kid friendly," Bo said.

"It surprised me. No one had told me about Clee. I realize I'm not around but..."

"C wanted to, but wasn't sure you'd get his message since you were halfway to another galaxy. He should have sent it, anyway."

"I got a message from Ian. He could have told me then."

"You know, Kneffs. They don't take their relationships as seriously as you Earth girls do. Probably why he didn't tell you about Kannika, either."

I sighed. "I still think about some things much like an Earth girl."

"Harry been good to you?" Bo asked.

"Yes, he has. He understands me. Having all that info he gathered about Earth has made it easier."

"He had an affection for Earth from the beginning. Did he tell you he first visited in the 1400s, Earth time?"

"Yes. I found his memories of all his visits. Amazing. We've had long talks about that time. He actually met Titian! Incredible."

"I hear talking. I need some of that coffee drink, Bo." Kannika entered the kitchen. She looked androgynous, with small breasts and small hips, about my height, short white hair against blue-black skin. She had a translucent wrap on and nothing underneath. My eyebrows shot up. Bo silently shook her head.

"You must be Claire. Your granddaughter is a pest. Last night, she came into my room to tell me you were here."

"Woah, there! You hit me with *that* before any introduction? You order Bo around AND have some disparaging remarks about my granddaughter? I don't care who you are or what you do. You are a guest here, no matter how many times you've slept with Ian. You respect this house and the people in it, and that includes the androids here."

"Or what?"

"You do not know what I can do. Do not frack with my family."

Kannika emitted a high-pitch shriek, at which point I slapped her. She stopped and stared at me She ran down the opposite hall, calling out Ian's name.

Harry entered as she left with fury on her face. He turned and watched her go.

"Oh, my dearest, my sweetest. Stirring up the hornets' nest I see," he said. "Good morning, Bo. How goes it?"

"Hello, Harry. The usual. Wherever that *thing* goes, trouble follows."

Clee came bouncing into the kitchen.

"Geegee, what happened to Kannika? She was screaming and crying and throwing things around. Opa Ian couldn't get a word in."

Ian, C, and Iryna walked into the kitchen. Ian tried explaining that Kannika was under a lot of stress. The premiere was in five days.

I interrupted him. "I don't care what excuse she has. You do not say what she said about my granddaughter, and you do NOT talk down to androids. Maybe Harry and I should stay on the *Houdini* until the concert."

"That is unnecessary. She'll be staying in Alpha City near the concert hall. I can shuttle back and forth. The symphony needs some fine tuning, anyway. I don't think slapping her was appropriate, though, Claire."

"Really, Ian, and how was I to prevent her from shattering all the surrounding glass?"

"Okay, okay, I get it. It just wasn't how I hoped you two would meet."

"Me neither. Harry and I will stay for the concert, but after that we will leave for Earth."

"Okay, well, I'm off to take her to the city. I'll see you for the evening meal?" Ian hurried down the hall.

"Oh, Geegee. Please, don't leave. You just got here, and I wanted to show you stuff. I started painting and I take pottery classes and... and..." Clee cried.

"Honey, sweetie, we can do things this week. I would love to see your paintings!" I said.

'Maybe she could come spend some time on Earth?' Harry subvocalized to me. I did a mental shrug and said, 'Let's see how this week pans out.'

The grown-ups looked at each other and burst out laughing.

"Mom, you slapped her? Wish I was here to see that!" C exclaimed.

"Do you want me to play it back for you, C?" Bo replied.

"Maybe later," Iryna said as she looked down at Clee. "As you can tell, we're not fond of her. We tolerate her because of Ian. There have been times I wanted to slap her myself."

"Oh, my darling dearest. I'm surprised you didn't clock her," Harry said.

"Yeah, I thought about it, but knew I'd lay her out for days. Didn't want to have the diva missing her opening. I dunno, Harry, I never would have done that as a human. Another bad influence of yours."

He grinned. "But you *are* human, just in a nonconformist body. And as startling as the act was, it was the only choice you felt you had. Talking to Kannika wouldn't have done any good."

LATER THAT DAY, Harry, C, Clee and I walked up to the observatory. It surprised me to see they had tidied it up. All of Ian's father's notebooks were placed on a shelf. There was a drape over the telescope. Clee ran outside to pick the wildflowers growing nearby and Harry and C talked energy tech. I was content to watch Clee flit from flower to flower.

I was still trying to wrap my head around being a grandmother. I thought that, at first glance, she looked human, but, of course, she wasn't. There may be a few human DNA strands floating around inside of her. I hope they serve her well. I should go pick flowers with her, but I enjoyed just watching her, her subtle movements, the way she examined each flower before she picked it. She cocked her head slightly to the left, just like I had seen Ian do so many times. She had those long Kneff fingers. No feathers sprouting from her head, only curls from her granny. She skipped inside and presented me with the bouquet. I got misty-eyed and gave her a big hug.

"They are beautiful, Claireena. Thank you!"

She smiled, then looked troubled. "Geegee, are you okay?"

"Yes, sweetheart. That was so very thoughtful of you. I am so thrilled and sorry I wasn't here at the start of your life. I regret that."

"It's okay. I felt like I knew you, even though you weren't here. Mom and dad shared all the videos of you with me. I read all about Earth and its history. Can I visit there one day?"

"Yes, of course. Maybe after the concert. Harry and I are

heading there then, and I think your dad is, too. Something about doing some energy research."

Clee threw her arms around me and whispered in my ear, "I love you, Geegee."

I got misty-eyed again.

As we walked back to the house, the first of Pi's messages came through. He had finished analyzing the Maratheusians' files and found some promising energy technologies. He wanted to consult with C about it, as there were several references to energy sources and materials that he did not immediately recognize. Pi had suggested they get together and offered to go to Alpha. C sent an immediate reply, inviting him to Alpha. C was thrilled and spent the rest of the day poring over the files.

I contacted Mike and asked if he'd mind giving Clee a ride around the planets in the system. He had been orbiting Alpha with not much to do. She and I transported up, and he took us on a tour. I had never seen the gas giant Gamma, so we headed there. It was as large as Jupiter, with a blue tinge to it. It had fifteen moons circling it. Two had research outposts on them. We swooped in towards Epsilon and Delta. Mike landed on Delta, and I took Clee to the house where I had stayed after my encounter with the wormhole. I showed her the studio I used, and the earth flora planted around the house. We walked down to the pier. There was a bow wave and just a dorsal fin above the surface coming toward us. We sat at the end of the pier. Suddenly, a large orca leaped into the air and came crashing down on the water. I heard that familiar laugh. Tilly's head popped up, and she waved hello.

"Hello, Clee, I am Tilly. I hope you didn't get too soaked!

Your Geegee and I became good friends when she first came here. She told me she would try to bring you here and I am so glad she did. I am an orca, one that came here a long time ago. Harry brought my family and other orcas here. We are hoping to one day to go back to our homeworld."

"Geegee told me about you, but I didn't think I'd ever meet you. I am so happy," Clee said.

"Harry said that they are going to move you and everyone else back to earth, starting in a couple of weeks. We're heading back there after the concert. I plan to take Clee and her dad with us. Iryna has an expedition she is planning, so she'll be staying here. C and another ship and Harry hope to get some research done on 'new' energy," I said with air quotes included. "How are you doing?"

"Good, I knew about the transfer coming. There are a few that are considering staying here. We've talked about it."

"When you get back to earth may I visit you?" Clee asked.

"Of course, we can have some fun!" Tilly replied.

We visited awhile longer, trading stories, making Clee laugh. It was late in the afternoon when we transported up to Mike and headed back to Alpha. It was near dinnertime when we arrived back at the house. Ian was there, but no Kannika. He mumbled something about her needing rest before the big day. Everyone did a mental sigh of relief.

Clee and I spent the next two days visiting the botanical gardens and museums. The Alpha Art Museum had two of my paintings. Clee asked intelligent questions about painting. She confessed she often came here just to look at mine. I took her to the markets and got her some of the special paints that I had used.

The day of the concert arrived. Ian spent most of the

day at the concert hall and then home for a couple of hours of rest, only he wandered around the house or fiddled with his instruments.

"Nervous?" I asked. I found him in the music room, sitting in front of the keyboards. He smiled briefly.

"Actually, I was thinking of Kannika. These last few days have been trying with her. I never realized just how demanding she can be. She lashed out at me a few times, complaining that the obahorns were drowning out her singing. They weren't."

"About her. I am sorry about slapping her. I reacted, and it was wrong."

"Bo told me later what had happened. I gather my family is not fond of her. And I'm wondering myself."

"Oh, Ian! If she makes you happy, that is all that matters."

"She did at first, but now... I'm not so sure. Anyway, Harry makes you happy?"

"Yes, yes, he does."

"Aren't we a pair? Android and almost-android," Ian said. "I've never regretted you. C is a wonderful son!"

"He is!" I said.

THE CONCERT WAS SPECTACULAR. The music was flawless and very moving. Kannika's singing was just beautiful. Her range was incredible; the emotion flowed from her voice. At the end, there were fireworks and a standing ovation that lasted for several minutes. Clee presented an enormous bouquet of Alpha flowers to Kannika. She accepted them graciously and even smiled slightly at the child.

There was a reception afterwards. People hovered near

Ian and the diva. So many species, some I didn't initially recognize. Harry and I walked the periphery of the room; I made eye contact with Ian. He was beaming. I found Clee with her mom and dad, and we agreed to head back to the house.

True to our words, Harry and I prepared to depart. Harry housed Mike in one of the *Houdini* bays. We checked systems and prepped for star flight. C and Clee would spend some time on Earth with us. Pi would meet C there. Iryna had an expedition to a newly discovered planet just beyond RA space. It was a general survey team with a geologist, chemist, archeologist, and the exobiologist. It was mid-day when Ian arrived back at the house. We informed him of our plans and said our goodbyes. Iryna hugged her daughter and kissed her husband. I couldn't have asked for a better partner for C.

With that, we transported to the Ship and entered alt.-space. Harry wanted Clee to have the full experience of space flight. He would drop into ordinary space to show her some phenomena: nebulas, pulsar stars, rogue planets, groups of stars, whatever. Clee asked intelligent questions and Harry replied in kind. She was more interested in the Ships and peppered him with questions. She impressed him, and Harry captivated her. Dare I say she has a bit of a crush?

With the dropping in and out of common space, it took us close to an Earth month. During that time, C and Pi communicated via vidphone. Pi arrived before us and orbited Earth after touring the system with *Sputnik*. Pi's avatar looked fairly human but in an ancient Greek way: dark curly hair with a trim beard, that Greek nose, muscular build, six feet. He reminded me of the Riace Warriors, only wearing some non-Greek clothing. I found out later he used them as inspiration. Harry had told him of my affection for Ancient Greek art.

We arrived in system and headed straight to Earth. The *Houdini* orbited Earth as we transported down in Mike. He used his VTOL engines and landed close to the gulf coast house. The droids had opened it up and added two rooms for C and Clee. Their rooms opened to a screened-in porch wrapping around the side of the house. It was early spring; azaleas were blooming in white and magenta colors. There were vases of flowers from the LGM. They knew me well. I hadn't realized how much I missed this place. It was nice to be home.

Deera and Larina greeted us. We introduced everyone around. There were refreshments; Clee enjoyed the lemonade. Everything was status quo. Larina took C and Clee to their rooms.

"Harry, I think Clee might have a small crush on you," I remarked.

"Yes, I kind of picked up on that. Smart girl, she has good taste in men," he said, "Just like her granny."

"Hey! Watch it, bub! Deera, no cat following you?" I teased.

"Funny you should say that. I got a report from Alex that they found a baby cheetah. They were looking for the mom but haven't had any luck. Alex tried having another mom cheetah care for him, but she rejected him. We think his mother may have abandoned him. The kit is small and has a short tail. Right now, we're caring for him at the Sanctuary. He's doing good. Should we bring him here?"

"No, I'd really like him to stay in the wild, but not alone. He'd never survive. We can keep him in the Sanctuary with the other orphans," I replied.

"Oh, one other thing. The Giganordudu have requested

to do research and set up an outpost on Titan with the goal of terraforming the satellite. I replied you had the final decision on that. I mentioned that there was life on the moon and their plans may not be possible," Harry said.

"Yeah, no, even though there are only microorganisms on it, no terraforming and no outpost. We have some droids on Titan doing research, yes?"

"Yes, Iryna's initial research continued after she left. There were molecules and one-cell organisms forming. It now has a multitude of various organisms, some multicellular. The Gigs can go somewhere else. Neptune maybe?" Deera suggested.

"See what alternatives we can give them. Why do they want to come all the way here? Surely, there are other places in RA they could use."

A light dinner was served: shrimp po'boys, dressed, a glass of white wine and Angelo Brocato's spumoni. I caught the shrimp in the Gulf, and we grew the lettuce and tomatoes in the kitchen garden. Some ingredients for the spumoni had to be refigured, but the cream, sugar, and nuts were locally sourced. I was so glad Harry could enhance my ability to enjoy food. The love of food was in my genes, especially growing up near New Orleans.

"Harry, do you know why the Gigs want to put an outpost here in the Solar System?" I asked between bites of my sandwich.

"Not offhand. I'll beam a message to Ian and see if he has any insight into it. I can use the new tachyon communicator Pi installed. It only does audio or text right now. But it is faster than light so we should get an answer quickly. I had a receiver installed in his house and this one. All Ships and RA governments will have them. I have a droid team taking care of it."

Pi transported down to say hello. The *3.1415* was orbiting Earth and the moon. He and C would start work tomorrow. Harry would contribute from time to time as he also would check on the other projects going on in the Solar System.

CHAPTER 5
INTERLUDE ON EARTH

I t had been a few days now on Earth and everyone seemed to have settled in. Clee was enjoying the beach on the Gulf. I showed her Minnie and the other cats' grave. She picked some flowers for it. She met Tilmir, one of the LGM, when he came with bouquets. They talked about flowers and growing things. She and Tilmir were the same height. We spent the day filling vases and setting them out in various places.

As I placed vases of flowers around the house, I noticed Pi staring at me. I sent him a snarky message: 'Like what you see?' He turned his head away from me at first, then started laughing.

"I had forgotten you were an avatar for a moment. Your movement is so... um... organic!" he said.

"That is the best compliment you could have given me." I smiled.

Harry was leaving to check on things in the outer system. Of course, he 'heard' the whole thing. He was chuckling as he walked down the hall to the kitchen. He planted a kiss on my cheek, looked at Pi, and shook his head. "Careful, she can rip that head right off your android body.

"I'll be back in a couple of days. C and Pi can get the energy research started. Message me if you need any extra insight," he said and with that, he transported up to his Ship. I always found it disconcerting when he did that. One second he's there, then he's not. Most RA species frown on the instantaneous transporting unless there is an emergency. People just didn't want other people showing up in their abodes unless they had an advanced warning, and it was for a good reason.

C and Pi commandeered my farmhouse table. They moved the chairs to the side, and set up several terminals and monitors on it. They also had some blueprints of various configurations of engines and other devices. It was old-fashioned, but seeing all the potential candidates together helped with the visualizations. They had a large screen behind the table where they could type or write various formulas on it.

I hoped they wouldn't make a mess. I slightly offended Pi, and C promised no junk-food wrappers or half-smoked cigarettes in an overflowing ashtray. We grinned at each other. He had studied Earth culture well.

I gathered our things and got ready to have Mike take Clee and me to Alexandria to see the museums. I told Pi and C good luck and we left. Clee had fun talking to Mike on the ride over. She asked him about the M-droids and he launched into a discussion about them, starting with their origins. Clee, as usual, asked intelligent questions She had trouble understanding why droids were not treated the same as everyone else. She scored a few points with that.

Mike landed next to the museums, and we went inside. She had a laugh seeing Reedmer and me as holograms. We spent the morning walking through the various Earth habitats and holograms of animals. There were displays of the various cultures through time and outlines of their histories. Clee took an interest in Chinese history. There were four of the terracotta warriors on display, as well as a few scrolls. I wished we could have saved them all.

We had a light snack in the café in the museum. There were various foods from all over RA. Clee had a Fluton salad that had three kinds of nuts sprinkled over the greens. There appeared to be small chunks of fruit along with some goat cheese. She got a lemonade. There was a refig unit for anyone who wanted something not on the menu. The menu choices, however, were fresh.

That afternoon, we visited the art museum. We wandered around at first, taking in all the galleries and displays. There was a room towards the back of the museum that was opened. I peeped in and a droid was working on a large cloth. Clee and I stepped in and said hello. The droid was carefully restoring a Kente cloth. He was gently repairing the holes in it. He looked up and blinked several times as we walked into the restoration lab.

"You must be Claire. I am honored to meet you. My name is Bert."

"Nimbo told me about the excellent work you have done here. This is my granddaughter, Clee. You are not the only one here, are you?"

"At the present, yes. We are having trouble finding the materials to restore several of the pieces. Ernie and Oscar have gone to scour the ruins to see what they can find. We have all the information to do the work just short of materials."

I laughed. "I see you've delved into some American culture. Your names."

"Yes, we are quite fond of *Sesame Street*. It seems to reflect the goodness of humans."

"Couldn't you just refigure the materials that you need?" Clee asked.

"We talked about that but felt we wanted to make everything as authentic as possible. If we must refigure it, we try to make it as close as possible to the original. We are also having trouble repairing some of the Chinese scrolls. We are looking into the various inks that were used. It is time consuming and sometimes tedious, but we enjoy the work, especially when the work is completed and placed on display."

"Thank you for your hard work. Everything looks great," I said, "I especially liked the gallery with all the human figures. It surprised me to see some Benin bronze heads. I take it the ivory is fake?"

"Of course, we found some pictures of the Benin Oba and his court standing those. Most of the ivory we found was in poor shape because of the bombings. We hope we can find other African art to fill a gallery. I think we have enough for a separate Chinese gallery but would like to include other Asian countries but we have not found enough artwork yet. *Dogon* has helped establish an archeology unit to roam earth looking for more artwork. We are fortunate that much information was saved. We have a dedicated archivist scouring the files. He is not here today, though. His name is Grover. He sometimes goes out with the team to help locate sites to dig or museums to look for. There are many smaller museums that we have not gotten to yet. We initially concentrated on the large museums and even those we go back to. The basements of those museums hold treasures as well. It is just a matter of looking for them."

I thanked him again, and we left Bert to his work. Clee and I talked a bit about the influences of Earth culture on the droids as we wandered through the galleries. She asked me if the earth references bothered me.

"It's not that it bothers me, but it is strange. I mean, there must be other cultures that have just as fascinating cultures as Earth. Yet, I haven't seen any influences to the extent there is of Earth. I dunno, is it a tragic story that has captivated people?"

"Opa Ian says it's because of Uncle Harry. He started long ago inviting the various animals to come with him to Delta. The Ships had transformed Delta into a miniature Earth. The plants were easy to transport. Over time, different species took Uncle Harry up on his offer. From what I read, Earth in the twentieth century had pollution problems and more and more animals left." Clee said.

"There are several species that went extinct that he saved. He's proud of that. His plan was to return them to Earth once things were better. Harry did a wonderful thing. I look over Earth and gasp at how beautiful things are here." I replied.

"Mom thinks it is because of the biodiversity here. Ever the scientist, Mom. Other planets are not as diverse."

"You realize there's a bit of humankind in you from me?" I asked.

"Oh, Geegee, yes, I do. It is the reason I am so fascinated by it all. Especially seeing everything up close. Seeing a picture of Earth is just not the same."

"You know this is not how Earth looked to me when I lived here. There were lots of large cities. True wilderness was limited to national parks. Animals were killed for trophies. Extensive areas of earth and ocean had trash strewn over it. It made me sad. Some people tried to do good, but I don't think it was ever enough," I sighed.

"Geegee, I didn't mean to make you sad."

"Oh, you haven't. I am glad someone had the forethought to save part of it. I've asked Harry if he thought we were doomed no matter what, but he denied it. He saved so much of Earth's life just because he wanted to. Apparently, he's done that with other planets. I guess Earth was/is a novelty?"

"Yeah, I guess so," Clee laughed.

We saw three Classical Greek bronzes that had been pulled from rubble. They graced the entrance to the gallery of human form. The Zeus/Poseidon was front and center, with the Riace warriors on either side of him. There were two more terracotta warriors and Rodin's The Thinker. Strange to see works of art I had studied in art history. Clee was excited to see the few Monet and Matisse paintings. One of my favorite paintings, *Bucket of Water* by Susan Rothenberg, was hanging in the twentieth century gallery after it had received a meticulous cleaning. We wandered around until I got a message from C.

Back at the house, work had progressed. C and Pi reviewed the information they had from the Maratheusians looking specifically at their applications for energy use. Their engines mostly used matter/antimatter as a fuel. They were exploring the possibility of using dark energy but hadn't gotten too far with it. Fortunately, Pi had access to all Ships' data regarding dark energy and gravity. Ships referred to it differently, but Pi thought 'dark' was just as good as any nomenclature for the phenomena. They studied their matter/antimatter specs. Ships had toyed with it, but after three ships blew themselves up, mind maps included, they stopped that research. Pi dug up those files and sent them to C's neural web. They spent the next two hours discussing the information. They looked at the dark sources. There was an abundance of it throughout the universe. Ships had determined that dark matter was, in fact, a particle that Earth scientists were on the verge of discovering when the 'war' broke out. They contacted 21-5 and asked if the M-droids could develop both engines and craft for the dark matter. He offered to send 'Redclay', a droid that specialized in energy production.

"Redclay? That is a very Martian name," C said.

"He wanted a distinct name. Oh, he is bipedal but has four arms. He can store two of them within his body. They are tools to help with different tasks. He's also very red," 21-5 said.

"No problems. I'm used to dealing with different species. But thanks for the heads up."

That afternoon Redclay arrived. The newest droid shuttles were quite fast. He greeted C and Pi, his extra two arms stored away. His voice was synthetic; his eyes extended and contracted like a variable camera lens. He had a deep terracotta-red metallic glint on his body. There was no mistaking what he was. He shared what information he had on energy sources, containers and engines for them.

"As you can see, M-droid technology focuses more on the manufacture of things. Our solar sail was a hit with some of the inner planets of systems. We don't usually delve into theories and abstract thinking. But there are a few of us who do, like myself."

"Here is all our research on dark matter/energy. It is still far away from anything practical," C said.

"What you refer to as 'dark energy and matter', are they related?" Redclay asked.

"Not really. Those are terms the Earth organics used.

The dark implies they don't really know what it is. The connection is tenuous. Dark matter only interacts with gravity and slows down the expansion of the universe. Dark energy seems to make the universe speed up as it expands from the early formation of it. It is called the Big Bang," C replied.

"Earth organics and their nomenclature. Quirky!" Pi remarked.

"Are there any other sources of energy you are considering?" Redclay asked. "Harry mentioned the Ships had tried to develop matter/antimatter as a source for fuel but didn't have much luck with it. I can review that as well. The shielding for the tanks needs to be very strong. I'm pretty sure I can change the specifications and come up with a good engine design. Would that work?"

"We got info from the Maratheusians about antimatter fuel. There were a couple of things I hope you could look at. They mention an exotic material but don't say specifically what it is. Also, the specs on their engines are bizarre. C and I are trying to make sense of it. Something seems to be lost in translation," Pi said.

"I've pulled up the info for the Ships'engine designs. Does it make sense to have one energy source for different engines? I'm thinking about winking vs. sub-light vs. FTL. Let's see what we can find," C offered.

"Ideally, it would be great to have just one fuel. But since we use the engines for different ways of traveling, we may be stuck with two or three different fuels," Redclay said.

With that, the three of them pored over math equations, molecules and atoms, types of EM and the sources for them. They scribbled away on the whiteboard or screens of the computers. After several hours, they came up with a solution and needed to test it. They agreed they would go to Mars for this. One problem was containment of the fuel; Mars was much better suited for this. No problem if something explodes. They could test far enough away from any habitation to cause any damage. They also had access to the M-droids' fabrication processes.

C informed me of their plans and Clee and I headed home from the museums. She wanted to tell her dad about her visit. It was nice talking "Art" to someone. I missed that. It was enjoyable to read all the comments about the artworks. Each species in RA had a different view on art: some considered it frivolous and didn't have any visual art; others indulged in it wholeheartedly. I had only myself.

"I messaged Tilly and we're going to go visit her tomorrow. Clee can stay with me while you work. Have you heard from Iryna?"

C replied, "Yes. They have just arrived on the planet and were setting up their base camp. She sounded excited. Clee got to spend some facetime with her last week. She's busy so no surprise there. Clee, you have fun with Geegee. I might be busy these next few days, but you can call me anytime."

"What about mom? Can I call her?"

"Wait until Uncle Harry gets back. You can use his fancy new communication system to contact her."

With that, C hugged and kissed his daughter. C, Pi and Redclay transported up to Mike.

"That always gets me when they do that," Clee said.

"Me too. Have I told you about *Star Trek*?"

Clee shook her head. I smiled and launched into a dissertation on it. I could just have Clee access it through Knowledge but telling her about it was much more fun. We planned to watch a few episodes after dinner.

The next day I took Clee to see Tilly. We landed near the droid base in southern Norway. The sun was sparkling on the water and there were a few puffy clouds. There was a slight, cool breeze.

I checked in with the two droids working there, Larina and 1246. We walked down to the pier that extended over the rocky coast. Waiting near the end of it was an orca. She slapped the water and sprayed us. I heard that familiar laugh.

"Tilly, you never stop playing, do you?" I laughed. "I'm guessing you are happy being here?"

"Hello, Clee, good to see you. I see you dressed for the water." Both of us had on the latest models of M-droid wet suits. The suits maintained a certain temperature for comfort depending on the species. One still got wet, but it was all part of the experience.

Tilly swam up to the end of the pier, rose, and waved a pectoral fin at Clee. She gasped, then laughed. She laid down on the pier and touched Tilly's head. Tilly responded by rolling her head.

"Oh, please, may I ride on your back? Is it okay? Geegee said she used take rides on you."

"Yes. Geegee would whoop and holler for me to go faster. We can take it slow. Melvin can take you, Claire. He's from another pod originally, but has stayed with us. He likes older women. Hehe!"

"Tilly! Hello all!" Melvin surfaced to the side of the pier, and I climbed on his back. Tilly took off with Clee, clinging to her dorsal fin. Melvin and I followed. I wasn't worried about Clee falling off. The suits had a special mechanism that inflated should we fall into the water and need help.

We swam to the nearby fiord. Tall mountains hovered over the glittering deep blue water. The orcas swam just under the surface, next to each other, rising occasionally to catch a breath. It reminded me of the carousels I had ridden as a child. The gentle rhythm was soothing. I pointed out to Clee some puffins nesting high on the mountains. She seemed mesmerized by it all. Seagulls dipped and swirled in the gentle wind. Further up the fiord, there appeared to be a bird of prey.

The sun dipped lower in the sky, so we headed back to the outpost. It was late afternoon and time for the orcas to help round up some herring for dinner. We bid the orcas farewell. Clee was quiet on the walk back; she didn't want to leave. We undressed in silence and sat at a small kitchen table, sipping on some hot chocolate. Finally, Clee looked at me with mournful eyes and exclaimed, "That was amazing, so, so, amazing, Geegee. Your Earth is wonderful!" and burst into tears.

"Oh, my sweet girl, you can visit anytime!" I gave her a hug.

We spent a few more days there. The droids showed us a nest of the white-throated dippers and a puffin colony. They monitored birds and other fauna in the area. They also kept track of the aquatic life in the north Atlantic. There was another droid team on Greenland that helped with that.

Clee and I hiked several trails, one leading to the top of a mountain overlooking the ocean. In the distance, there were some ominous dark grey clouds and a distant rumble. The wind picked up, so we hurried back and made it just as the clouds discharged their rain. It was a heavy downpour but didn't last long.

While I waited out the storm at the outpost, I got a message from Harry. He was at the Gulf Coast house. He had checked in with C and things were going well: only two explosions so far. I told Harry about our adventures and would be there soon. I mentioned to him that Clee wanted to talk with her mom. Harry said C had told him and would set it up for Clee when we returned.

We said our goodbyes to the droids and headed back. I flew over to Scotland and then down the East coast, heading inland over New York. Even after all these years, I could still see vestiges of brown spots around where cities once were. Harry had told me the droids were still working on cleaning it up. New York had sustained heavy bombardment along with Moscow and Tokyo. I had a moment of sadness, but it passed quickly as we flew over the green forests of Appalachia. Harry greeted us as we landed, and Clee launched into telling him of the adventures we had.

He signaled Iryna's base camp but got no answer. The signal was strong; there was no interference. After several tries, Clee sent a short video and said they would try later. Harry subvocalized it was unusual for no one to respond, as each team member had portable communicators capable of picking up his transmission. I thought perhaps there was some glitch on their end. It was worrisome.

Over a meal of trout almandine and wine, Harry told me about the Giganordudu's request to establish a colony in the solar system. They had made several requests to Deatine. She explained they had to go through me. It puzzled me why they wanted to come all this way as the solar system was out of RA space and far away.

"I asked Ian about it, and he found out that a faction of Gigs is considering leaving RA. The Gigs had a dispute with the Zanderthums. It seems they both lay claim to a system on the border of RA and Zanderthum space. The Gigs had been surveying the area and found this system that had three planets. Two had a methane atmosphere. They began surveying the two planets when the Zanderthums showed up, claiming all three. Deatine ruled in favor of the Gigs for the two and the third for the Zanderthums. The Gigs don't trust the Zanderthums and protested to no avail. What makes matter worse is that there are veins of a rare mineral on one of the Gig planets. They worked out a plan for the Zanderthums to mine the mineral and to share the profits. A faction of Gigs was not happy and located here. It is understood that they won't be in the RA. *Dogon* and *Sputnik* have agreed in principle to help them. They would like to set up a station orbiting Neptune as it has the ingredients to sustain them. They would do their own research but offered to help with any projects in the outer system. There are seventy-two of them, so we're not talking of a large contingent. The Gigs may seem odd, but I've never heard of any problem with them."

"Sure, why not? It'll be good to have someone out there."

"Geegee, you'd look good with a crown. Maybe you could dress up like Empress Wu. She sounded tough!" Clee said.

"Yes, she was. I'm not an Empress and I don't want a crown. I don't enjoy making these decisions about other people's lives except for Earth. At least, people are respecting the system and asking permission."

"That was a decree made by Ian when he was Prime. He was adamant that anyone wanting to visit or research or just fly-by had to check with you or me or himself if we weren't around. Ian was the one who limited the number of ships that can go to Earth. He's very protective of it," Harry said.

After dinner, we took a walk along the Gulf Coast. I told Clee she needed to go to Florida's Emerald coast. It was especially nice now that all the tall condominiums were gone. Nimbo and Tulla were restoring parts of the beach that had eroded from a storm. Harry had offered to place weather control systems around the planet, but I wanted to keep it as natural as possible. There were domes that activated for protection.

Clee was tired and headed to bed. She wanted to read more about Empress Wu and orcas. I was glad she had an interest in Earth.

Harry and I sat on the screened-in porch. The last rays slowly sank in the west. I missed having a cat.

"I didn't want to say anything in front of Clee, but should we be worried that we can't raise Iryna's expedition?"

"C said that sometimes it would be a few days before he'd hear from her, but this is what? Almost three Earth weeks and he is concerned. I talked to Deatine about it and RA was considering sending a ship or two out there. I suggested they may send a small military contingent, since we do not know what has happened. *Torgun* offered to be a part of the flotilla."

"*Torgun* is in the Milky Way? How did it turn out for the Ukarish?"

"They won, but have suffered massive devastation. They asked to join RA and the ministers have agreed. The RiRa were stripped of all their military hardware and weapons and have made reparations. We isolated them from the rest of the planets."

"Good to hear. So, when do we leave?" I asked.

CHAPTER 6
OFF COURSE

"Now, unless you have any objections, there is an LGM that has requested to come with us. He would like to survey the area for any biological specimens. I thought it would be fine since it is Hymir."

"Of course, he can come! I can catch up on what has been going on with them. This system we're headed to, how long?" I asked.

Harry replied, "Hymir is on board. I configured an indoor garden, complete with a hammock for him. He should be fine there. I stored Mike with the other smaller starcraft. He asked, and I agreed. We may need him at some point.

"Calculations show the fastest, even with winking, will be nine days. It is on the other side of RA space out of the Milky Way galaxy proper. The system is in between it and the Sculpture Galaxy. We have upgraded the engines with some Maratheusian tech to improve efficiency, but it is still far. We're actually using a new type of engine that C, Pi and Redclay designed. I'm eager to see how they work."

"I see where all the tests were successful. Who named it the dark engine?"

"Pi did. A nod to quirky Earth nomenclature."

"So they worked all the kinks out? I'd hate to break down somewhere and have to call roadside service. Might be awhile before they come."

"I see you haven't lost your sense of humor. We installed another tachyon communicator with the M-droids, so that'll help. The androids have all the info on it so we should be good. Clee is staying with C and Ian?"

"Yes, C initially wanted to go, but Clee convinced him otherwise. It would have been nice to have C here with us, but I am worried about what we might find. I'm glad Mike is with us, especially since we don't know what we are dealing with."

Hymir entered the bridge. "C said to tell you, Claire and Harry, safe journey and Clee said to please bring her mom back. Also, she loves you both."

"Good to see you. I just sent them a message saying we were leaving the system. When we get some time, I'll tell you about my visit to Venus5. Thanks, Hymir," I said.

"I got a report from Merrimun, but I'd love to hear your impressions," Hymir replied.

Shiva, *Torgun* and *Endtimes* headed out with them. A short period of rest followed the first wink so the new engines could restore the lost energy. Dark matter was apparently everywhere. The only drawback was the limit on how much dark matter they could store for the engines. Winking used most of it. The small convoy traveled into common space and then winked again. For the rest of the voyage, we flew in alt.space.

While we zipped along in alt.space, I asked Harry about the Ships that tried to find the beginning of the universe.

"Have you heard anything about *Labinder* and *AS125*? I was wondering if time would be reversed as you traveled backwards. I've looked through all the files we have concerning the beginning of the universe, but there is nothing definitive about any of it. You should be able to go back and see the beginning of the universe, yes? If you travel faster than light?"

"In theory, I guess you could. There are many factors involved and I just don't see how you could compensate for them all. The universe is expanding, so you'd have to consider that too. I understand where you are coming from, but it is all conjecture at this point. Ships have a similar 'Big Bang' theory but with some subtle differences. I think earth scientists called it a 'big bounce'. Anyway, *Labinder* and *AS125* wanted definitive proof. I don't think going to the beginning of our universe is possible from what I understand. I would think at some point the matter that is you would break down. You would just dissolve away, but who really knows?" Harry shrugged.

Torgun chimed in: "You haven't heard then? *AS125* finally sent a message. She is en route to M110, but her alt.engines were damaged, so she is only traveling at 47% efficiency. *Labinder* had pushed on further. *AS125* said they reached a region of space that was mostly plasma but heavy with hydrogen atoms. The heat was incredible, and the enhanced shielding was inadequate to withstand it. They couldn't go around it as it was an enormous area: several megaparsecs across. She turned back, but *Labinder* went on. About sixteen light years further in from where *AS125* had turned, *Labinder* broke apart from the heat. His last message was garbled and only part of the message came through. It was "hot... see ...begin... thing... fused... losing coherence." That was it. *AS125* could sense nothing of *Labinder* and assumed the heat destroyed his mind map."

"Was *AS125* able to transmit any data they may have gotten along the way?" I asked.

"Not sure, *AS86* and *AS105* volunteered to meet *AS125*. It will take her about a hundred years to reach M110 traveling at her current speed and that is assuming nothing goes wrong. The two Ships can wink and get there in about five years. Hopefully, there is some new information we can rummage through."

"I am sorry to hear about *Labinder* but glad *AS125* is still with us. It seemed like a baffling idea to me, but also a bit intriguing. I mean, what if you really could see the start of it all?" I replied.

"Yes, understand that *Labinder* was a bit, um... eccentric. He'd always conjure up wild ideas. He often talked about going to the end of the universe, but we convinced him that since it is expanding, he would never reach it," *Torgun* said.

"I remember the heated discussions we had with him. It took some talking, but he finally gave it up. He was a quirky personality, and I am going to miss all of his outlandish ideas," Harry said.

"Changing the subject, what do you expect about this rogue system of Iryna's?" I asked. We had received an initial report from the expedition with descriptions of the surface of the planet. Two moons orbited the planet. A belt of tropical forest was around the equator and a large prairie of grass on its largest continent. Areas of desert with blue-green vegetation lay along the fringes. Frequent rainstorms battered the lands, but they had set up base at the foot of a mesa somewhat protected from the storms. There are several caves nearby. They also described greenish-blue vegetation on top of the mesa. There was a stream that flowed into the valley that had the mesa on one side and, on the other, a mountain ridge that went for miles.

Hymir joined Harry and me in the observation room. I still smile when I see the Little Green Men. They had become loyal inhabitants of the Solar System and skillful stewards of the Venus planets throughout the galaxy and local group. It was decided by the LGM to refer to their terraformed planets as Venuses with numbers after it. I learned from Hymir that there were three planets beyond our local group that some of the LGM had headed to. They settled there, but because of the distance, our LGM had little contact with them. They were installing the tachyon communicators among them with M-droid help.

We talked about the greenish-blue vegetation mentioned in the initial report. There was more varied plant life on other parts of the planet, it seemed. Iryna's report gave a general description, but Hymir wanted to do a detailed survey of the plants and possibly take some samples with him back to Venus. He and the other LGM had set up large experimental greenhouses on Venus and Delta. They turned Delta into an experimental research farm with not only various plants but animals from different planets. The LGM had a presence with helping the RA exobotanists. There were also areas for various fauna, each being isolated and studied. When compatible, some animals were mixed with others from various planets. There were Earth animals that stayed on Delta. They used none of the Earth fauna for interbreeding. A bit of vanity perhaps, but with the extinction of earth life, I wasn't taking any chances. Hymir's knowledge of plant life was amazing. He and Harry talked about some large carnivore plants on a satellite of a system in the general area. Hymir had gathered two specimens on a previous trip. He was hoping to gather some new specimens.

Harry and *Torgun* started a new game of 3D chess. They had been looking forward to it. They played each other over the years, sometimes sending moves through messages if they didn't see each other. I could follow the game through Harry, but left him to it.

I wanted to review the message Iryna had sent. Nothing seemed wrong. The land reminded me a little of the southwest of North America on Earth. Red-brown rock, dusty. One could see the small stream in the valley in the distance with a strip of green, blue-green and yellow-green vegetation along both sides. There seemed to be a lack of animal life.

As we approached the system, we started getting strange energy readings. Harry couldn't pinpoint the source. It seemed to be all around the system. We dropped out of alt.space and cautiously approached the planet. The other three ships reported the same energy readings. Harry sent out a general call to the expedition. There was no answer. We all began scanning for the group. Along with Iryna were two Kneff technicians: med tech Pelu and lab tech Dontu. They were cousins. A Quozan archeologist named Lundamera, called Lund for short, and a Ca'keenie geologist called Oranorowani, or Oran, made up the rest of the group.

We increased our signal and broadcast on their individual terminals. Again, no answer. If they were dead, we would at least pick up their biological signs. Nothing; it was as if they never made it here, but there was evidence of the base camp. Harry zoomed in on it. There was the larger dome used as a lab, along with several smaller domes for habitats and storage. They had set the site under a large overhang and what appeared to be an entrance to a cave in the back of the overhang.

Shiva messaged she would orbit the planet, keeping sensors on full alert. Harry, *Torgun* and *Endtimes* prepared to descend to the planet. They agreed they would take the smaller shuttles down.

Suddenly, the energy readings spiked. There was a high-pitched whine; the sound was followed by a strong EM wind. It blew the Ships off course, millions of miles away. I had strapped myself into one of the control room seats. Harry had been walking in the corridor towards the control room. The Ship flipped end to end several times. Inertial dampeners tried to kick in but only stopped the flip and put us into a spin, all the while sending us goddess knows where. Hymir cocooned himself in his bed, riding it out. He had a gel-form cushion that conformed to his body and absorbed any force against it. Of course, it was an M-droid design. The whine of the engines wound down to a low hum. The Ship finally stopped rotating and was dead in the water. I called to Harry several times but got no answer. He was slumped down, leaning on the wall in the hallway. I turned him over, checked his energy packs. His eyes were dark, blank circles. I tried all the reset programs I knew, but to no avail.

I got him into our med bay. Harry had designed it for Ships' droids and organics. I put him on a table and connected him to the various sensors and monitors. His avatar body was on minimum energy output. I tried several more times to raise him to consciousness, but no luck. I needed to get the engines back online, but well... I never paid much attention to the inner workings of the ship itself. Yes, I could access the files and I did. But it is one thing to have the knowledge, it's another to use it in real time. There are so many finesses involved. I gathered as much of Harry's information and experiences as I could, but could not access all his personal files. I saw just how connected he was to his ship, or should I say, to himself. His avatar was the personification of the huge number of files, functions, experiences of the Ship itself. He had access to an enormous amount of information collected over thousands of millennia. It boggled my mind. Right now, I had to access the files for running the ship without his consciousness. I found those files and began opening them. There was a subfile marked 'AI' that opened automatically as I accessed more and more files.

"Hello. I am AI Harry. I understand there is a problem with avatar Harry?"

"Yes, yes. I can't get him back online. Can you?"

"Accessing information, one moment."

It was a long one moment, but he came back.

"The Ship was subjected to a violent force that pushed it well beyond the speed of light. It was not designed for the fourteen end-over-end flips. The Ship cannot take those stressors in ordinary space. I am limited in what I can do, but I will start system checks to get the dark matter engines working. That will give us some propulsion in ordinary space and allow for interior systems to come online. The hull did not suffer any damage."

"Do you know where we are?"

"Accessing information, one moment. We're out near the M33, or the Triangulum galaxy."

"Can you scan for the other Ships?"

"Accessing information, one moment. Yes, there is one not moving on the other side of the T-galaxy, minimum EM output. And there is one in alt.space heading towards us."

"A Ship? Can you identify it?"

"*17.*"

"Can you send a message?"

"Working. Speak and I'll transmit it."

"To ship *17*. This is the *Harry Houdini*. I am Claire. Something threw us off course and we have sustained damage to our engines. I cannot rouse avatar Harry. I have the AI working, appreciate any help."

"Avatar Claire, this is *17*. I am sending a smaller ship equipped with getting you back up and running. It should get there in about four hours. There is another ship that is not responding to our hails, the *Torgun*. I am traveling towards him. Was he with you?"

I explained to *17* what had happened and asked to scan for the other Ships. Our long-range sensors were glitchy. He would let me know what he found.

In the meantime, the AI and I went through systems trying to restore what we could. We had general environmental controls back up. Those were easy. It was the wink and alt.drives that were complicated. We started with the drives. They would allow us to enter alt.space. I could follow the steps all the way until the actual adding of energies to ignite the process that allowed the engines to start. There was a subtle balance that took some finessing, finessing I had no experience with. The AI coached me on the initial steps, but for the actual firing of the engines, it was up to me. I tried accessing his memories, but it seems the running of the ship was automatic and subconscious. I had to rely on the AI and his knowledge was limited. I had maintained my identity by not accessing the inner workings. I am not a Ship, nor do I ever want to be one and yet, here I am. I turned off all emotional responses, took a deep breath, not that I actually needed it, and began.

There were two instrument readouts I needed to focus

on: the amount and the balance of the flow of particles. Slowly, I added energy into the chamber; too much, too soon, and the engines would overheat and explode. So far, so good. A little more and I stopped. I must add them continuously at a slow pace, but these first few attempts were me understanding what was going on and just how delicate of a touch I should use. I began the very slow uptake, watching that the readouts stayed in the green.

Finally, I saw where the levels were over the black line that showed minimum energy for alt.space. There was enough dark matter for two jumps until it would have to be replenished. I hoped Harry would be back with me by then. It was still another two hours before the smaller ship would arrive, so I went down to our med bay to see what I could do for Harry. My biggest worry was his mind map. Was it still in there and how could I get it up and running?

The AI was little help with this. His role was to get the basic systems running. He had no access to the higher functions of the Ship, nor was he able to do anything about the wink drives. He could tell that those engines seemed to be undamaged but needed Harry to check them.

I entered the med bay and walked over to where he was still lying on the table. I got a low sensory reading from him, similar to the one when I went looking for him during the RiRa war.

So far, so good. There was a port on his back near the base of his head. That would hopefully get his thought processes going. I found the correct plug and connected it to him. Nothing at first. I opened wide all my senses and began calling his name. Emotions spilled over me. Regret, sadness, determination, and love—always love. Maybe the emotions would wake him. Nothing. Just a low hum emanating from him.

"Please, Harry, wake up. I can't do this. I can't navigate this 'alternative reality' without your guidance. I need you. Please... please..."

With that, a tear fell from my eyes. I got a chair and sat down next to him, holding his hand with my head on his chest. I sobbed.

And then I heard that heartbeat. It was faint but gradually got stronger. I lifted my head and looked at his face. Ever so slowly, he opened his eyes. He blinked, saw me, and smiled.

"Oh, my love, what happened? ... Ah, I see. Thank you for waking me and I see you got the engines online. I guess I am redundant," he said.

"No, no, you are not. Even with all my emotions turned off, I was still terrified about starting the engines. I just have your higher functions restored. I haven't gotten to the motor functions."

"No problem, see those green and orange lines? They connect here." His chest opened and his inner workings were exposed. There were two ports that I connected the lines to. Color coding made it easy.

Suddenly, he sat up and swung his legs over the side of the table. I pushed his legs open and wrapped my arms around him, kissing his chest. I dialed down the emotions now that he was with me again. A kiss, a very long, lovely kiss, and the lovely sound of that heartbeat.

"I'm so glad you did not blow me up. That would have been *most* unfortunate." He had that mirth in his voice.

I looked at him and laughed. He joined in and we hugged and laughed and kissed.

Hymir found us in the middle of our uproarious laughter.

"Are you okay?" he asked.

"Yes, yes, we are fine. Just a release of tension. How did your gel work?" I asked.

"Wonderful. I felt vibrations, but nothing more. Have to let the M-droids know when we get back to the Solar System," he replied.

"Ship *17*'s frigate is here requesting docking permission. Avatar Harry, I see you are back with us. I turn control of my systems over to you," AI Harry said.

"Thank you, AI Harry. You are a valuable member of my crew. Go to standby mode; control accepted."

"Avatar Harry, this is F-17. We just docked and can run system checks and do anything else you may need."

"We've started checks. I need to have the hull's structure scanned for micro fractures. I may need your help with the wink drives. They are offline."

"Yes, Harry, scanning begun. If we find any fractures, we can repair and/or notify you. Wink drive?"

"Yes, winking is what Claire calls the instantaneous jump drives."

While the frigate scanned the outer hull, Harry looked over the system for the wink drive. It was in good shape, though low on fuel. There were several areas of dark matter nearby to gather more.

We got a message from *Torgun* about an hour later. *17* found him and was helping with repairs. We would meet at a dark matter site as he needed energy for his wink drive, too.

Two hours later and everything was restored to working order. There were few fractures that didn't seem to pose any threat. Harry checked over the alt.drive. He said I did an excellent job. He opened up all the files on the engines to me. I still had little desire to probe the inner workings of the ship, but I knew now I needed to know how they worked.

He and the frigate got the wink drive back up. It had enough fuel for one wink. It would get him close to a dark matter pond. I think of them as pools of matter, seas, lakes, oceans of dark matter. Both large and small, they were everywhere.

Harry signaled *Torgun* we were heading there. He had a few minor repairs left. *17* signaled they were going back into the Triangulum galaxy. The frigate disengaged with Harry and flew to meet *17*.

"Thank you, *17*. Tell the other ships hello and thanks for those files. Never know when they might come in handy." The files contained information gathered from their time in the T-galaxy. Harry had given *17* all the info on the new engines. It intrigued him.

I held my breath as Harry engaged the wink drive. As I let it out, we were at a small pond of dark matter. Harry began gathering the fuel we needed. As we were finishing, *Torgun* arrived and started the same procedure. He and Harry analyzed what had happened when the wind blew us off course. They had sent out hails and messages to *Shiva* and *Endtimes* but got no response. It was worrisome.

With one wink, we got to the outer reaches of the Sculptor group. *Torgun* and Harry began scans of the area going as far as the edge of the Sculptor galaxy. They didn't want to call attention to themselves. Harry sent out a general message hoping it would not cause alarm. *Shiva* answered it. The wind had sent her only to the edge of the Sculptor galaxy. She had suffered minimal damage and had been circumnavigating the galaxy looking for them. She hadn't heard from *Endtimes*.

"I set a couple of buoys up on the other side of the

galaxy for all three of you, in case I was not near that space. So glad you are back. I kept a distance from the system but would do some passive scans of it. Nothing, no EM activity, no evidence of anyone."

"I think with the three of us here, we should try to head to the planet again. We need to find out what happened to the expedition. When we get close enough, we need to transport down directly. I'm thinking maybe they thought the Ships were a threat, whoever *they* might be," Harry said.

"We can have the Ships hold just beyond the system. Hymir, do you have an environmental suit? The atmosphere seems thin," Harry asked.

"Yes, I have one. It also protects from harmful rays and other potential dangers. The oxygen content in the atmosphere is thin, but the suit can provide extra oxygen and can balance the amounts. Another creation of the M-droids." Hymir nodded.

"I'm going to have Mike orbit the planet in case we need transport. I've also sent a message to Alpha informing them of our intentions and mishap."

Hymir commented that the force that hurled them reminded him of a species in his universe that had a similar defense for their planet. As far as he knew, the black hole of his universe had swallowed them up. He said that the species, the Poréthonians, were technologically adept. He described them as intelligent. They valued knowledge above all else, and were introverted, peaceful, but fierce if threatened.

"As more species wandered our universe, they came upon their system and tried to exploit them. Little did they know that while the Porés were peaceful, they had a violent past. They had fought several wars with interlopers and always won. Word got around to leave them alone. They helped us once when a group of Yunderfics tried to start trouble with us. The Porés took care of them. We had shared information with them on the enlarging black hole. They knew we were headed to this universe, but they thought they could destroy the hole. When we left, they signaled they were staying 'to fight' it."

"They sound like they would be good people to know," I said.

With that, we all beamed down to the base camp.

CHAPTER 7
MYSTERY

There was a steady wind and several grey clouds in the distance moving our way. We searched the camp and the immediate surroundings but saw no signs of anything unusual. We accessed different logs from the main computer. Just general observations of the surrounding area. There was talk of going to the top of the mesa at some point, but Iryna wanted to concentrate on the valley first. They noted a lack of any animal life. Their personal scanners were missing as well as a med kit and emergency survival kit. Did someone get hurt? Hymir thought it unusual that they had collected no specimens of the plant life near the camp.

The storm clouds were upon us. There were violent flashes of purple lightning, followed by loud cracks of thunder. We took shelter under the overhang as the clouds opened up. We could hear the water gushing in the stream below us. Near the back of the overhang was the opening of a cave. We checked it out as the rain was blowing into the shelter. It was dark at first, but we then noticed a faint greenish-yellow light glowing in the distance. We walked toward it. There was a tinkling sound, and the light grew brighter. The light and sound were coming from a portal or door of some sort. There seemed to be a force field across it. It flickered off and on, and the field was translucent. Near to it was a dropped scanner. It belonged to Lund, the Quozan archeologist.

"Any thoughts? Looks like they went into the portal," *Torgun* said. "Can't make out any details, but there seem to be some rocks near the opening on the other side."

"Went or forced to. I don't see how Lund would drop his scanner and not pick it back up. I wonder if whoever created the force that threw us is still around," Harry said.

"My scans show no complex organic life," Hymir replied.

"Agreed. So, do we go into this opening?" I asked. I was a little anxious about stepping into the unknown, but was curious about what was on the other side. I contacted Mike and asked him to orbit the planet and keep a watch on things. I wasn't sure if our communicators would work on the other side of the portal, so I told him to contact Ian and Alpha command if we didn't return in four hours.

"We all have handheld blasters and personal force fields. Set both to maximum and let's go." Harry grinned as he stepped into the opening.

We followed. There was a brief, disorienting moment, but it passed. The landscape was utterly strange. Two moons in the sky that were setting. A rocky terrain, no evidence of life as we know it. The sky was a violet blue that got lighter as the sun rose in the distance. The sun was a dull red and smaller than our own. In the distance, we saw the ruins of a small city. The buildings looked canted to one side. Opposite the rising sun was the black hole. It was far from the planet as it was small, but even that far away it seemed to have an adverse effect on the planet.

Holding our blasters in hand, we walked towards what looked like a small campsite. It belonged to the expedition. We found some bloody bandages mixed in with the survival equipment bag. We scanned it and found it was Ca'Keenie blood.

"Looks like Oran was injured. Maybe they went to that city looking for help," I said.

"I recognize this planet. This is the Porés planet. It is on the edge of a system that had four planets. There were three moons. I'm guessing the black hole ate one. I'm not seeing any signs of the expedition, nor of the Porés," Hymir said.

"Our instruments are going to be of limited use, as this is a different universe with different laws," Harry said.

"Yes, although your universe and ours are similar, which is why we chose it," Hymir said.

"Why didn't they just go back to our universe if Oran was injured?" I wondered.

"Maybe they didn't think she was hurt that bad. I'm getting faint distorted readings from that city. Can't tell if it is our people or not. Let's head in that direction," *Torgun* said.

We engaged our jet packs to save time. In a few minutes, we arrived in the city. We sent out a general message and got an immediate response. It was Iryna. We quickly located them in a small building just off a central square. Iryna was there, along with Oran and Pelu. Lund and Dontu were surveying the city. It looked recently abandoned.

Iryna hugged each of them and explained what had happened.

"We set up camp, had an evening meal, and started

the next day. It was an overcast day with some dark clouds in the distance. After our breakfast, it rained, steady, so we explored the cave. We found the opening. Oran went in first and almost immediately, we heard a scream from her. We all raced through the opening. Dontu grabbed an emergency survival pack. That must have been when Lund dropped his scanner. Oran was fighting a creature. It had long, grey-green hair, six legs, and razor-sharp teeth. The beast had a large, curved horn on its head and kept trying to pierce Oran with it. Have you ever seen a Ca'Keenie fight? She was a whirl of arms and legs. She battered the creature left and right and then spat acid onto the creature's face. It ran off. Oran had a gash in one of her arms. We wanted to go back, but she said it wasn't that bad. So, we bandaged it and gave her a broad-spectrum antibiotic and off we went. We had just gotten to the city when we noticed she wasn't looking well. She collapsed. We got her to this house, and she has been unconscious since then. That was three days ago. Lund, Dontu and I raced back to the opening and found we couldn't go through! We set up camp in this house. We sent out a general distress call on this side, hoping someone was still here. It doesn't seem likely. We've been going through the buildings, seeing if we could find anything useful. We found blankets and some water and food. They seemed acceptable by our readings from our scanners. We also had our ration bars with us. We had the survival pack, but we didn't know how long we would be here."

"Hello, Iryna, I am Hymir. I am originally from this universe, and I recognize this planet as belonging to the Poré. The creature you encountered sounds like a Beturnagin. Nasty animals. The Poré used their fur to make fabric.

Anyway, have you come across a dispensary or chemist, something that looked like medicine and such?"

"We found something that looked like a pharmacy. Lund, can you show him?" Iryna asked.

Lund nodded, and he and Hymir set off to find it. It didn't take long, and they came back with their backpacks filled with some bluish liquid, a salve of some sort, bandages and some red pills. There were several containers of what looked like water.

Hymir washed the wound with the blue liquid, cleaned it, and applied the salve. Oran moaned while Hymir wrapped the wound with the bandages. The bandages were infused with another medicine that would help in the healing.

"Beturnagins carry microbes that infect whoever is unlucky to come in contact with them. It is on their horn, claws, and teeth. The medicine I used can cure the infection, but I do not know if it will work on a Ca'Keenie. She should wake up in a couple of hours. She'll need to take those red pills for a week to get rid of the rest of the infection. We found some purified water. I hope this will work, if not…"

"When we didn't get any further reports from you, we knew something was wrong. C wanted to come, but Clee convinced him otherwise. There was a lot of crying. Did you encounter a force or wind that blew you away from the planet?" Harry said.

"No, nothing of the sort. There were some strange EM readings about sixteen klicks from the base camp. That was on our list to explore."

"We would have been here sooner, but some kind of force blew us away from the system. We need to figure out how to open up the portal again," Harry said.

"That black hole is not going away. I figure we have about twenty-three to twenty-eight hours before it consumes this planet," *Torgun* said.

"We need to head back to the opening now. Hymir, is there anything here we can use that you know of?"

"There may be a controller. I've seen the Porés use a handheld device to deactivate force fields."

"Hymir, you and *Torgun* look around here to see if you can find one, and we will head back to the opening. We have our blasters if the Beturnagin comes back," Harry said.

They made a stretcher to carry Oran. The small anti-gravity units worked well, and the rest of the group started back. We hoped *Torgun* and Hymir could find a controller or things would be grim.

CHAPTER 8
MYSTERY SOLVED

Meanwhile, in our universe, *Endtimes* finally came back online. He was in the opposite direction from Harry and *Torgun*. It was a region of space called Bootes Void, that Ships were not familiar with. There was a vague report of enormous creatures in the area.

He began assessing his damage. The wink drive was offline. There was structural damage to one engine and little energy left for the drives. He began repairs and sent out a general distress call. *Endtimes* scanned the area for any signs of planetary systems or sentient life. He widened his parameters to include any strange phenomena. He got a hit. A massive dark thing was creeping towards him. He received no information about it. He checked his sensors; they seemed to work.

Well, I'm dead in the water so I hope it is friendly, *Endtimes* thought.

He sent a greetings message in all the languages he knew. Nothing at first. But then a few minutes later, a message came back!

"Hello, Ship. I am a Galaxy Wanderer. That is also our species' name. You may call me Galwon Three. There are ten of us in this region of space. We like the areas of space that are voids. We have been all over the universe. How can I help you?"

Endtimes explained his predicament to Galwon. His biggest problem was energy sources. The repairs to the engines were going well. He asked if there were any energy sources nearby. *Endtimes* told him what he needed and Galwon said he could bring some fuel to him. It was not a problem.

Galwon was huge. *Endtimes* estimated his size was about seventy meters. He had a bluish tint with areas of deep purple. They were creatures born in space like the Ships, but the comparison ended there. The Wanderers procreated by a kind of mitosis, in that they doubled in size and then divided into two. The "offspring" had all the memories and experiences of the "parent". They avoided areas that had organics. They lived a very long time like Ships. Galwon told *Endtimes* of an encounter with a Ship, the *Heraclitus*. He was sorry to hear of her demise.

Another Wanderer arrived with fuel for engines. It transferred it to *Endtimes* easily. He started the process to get the engines back on line.

Galwon requested and *Endtimes* granted him more information about the RA and Earth. He was intrigued by Earth's steward, Claire.

"We had gotten some information from *Heraclitus,* but we did not know of this, Claire. Perhaps we could one day converse with her. Her situation is unique for organics, is it not?"

Endtimes replied, "Yes, she is the only one left of her

species. There were many Ships who felt it was not a wise decision to have an organic in an avatar's body. She is unique. Harry is, well, a rather atypical Ship. He felt it necessary to save her, as she was the last of her kind. And also, he fell in love with her."

Galwon glowed a brighter blue and the grey areas lightened.

"Yes, love, I can understand. We have a similar feeling. If any of us are in danger, we all rush to that Wanderer's help. We are formidable creatures."

"We have no information about you from *Heraclitus*," *Endtimes* said.

"That is because we asked her not to share that knowledge. We keep to ourselves and only reveal ourselves when we want."

"I am glad we have met on good terms. Perhaps, one day, we could have you meet Claire. I thank you, Galwon Three, for your generous help." With that, *Endtimes* entered alt.space.

After gathering enough dark matter, he winked back to the system. He saw the *Houdini* and *Torgun* Ships. They had had no contact with the group for three hours. *Endtimes* contacted Mike and asked if his avatar could transport over to him and then down to the planet.

"It is rather strange. I had all their signals and then suddenly, nothing. Their last communication was that they had entered a cave and there was some strange light coming from it. I've tried scanning the cave, but have only got some unusual readings deep within it."

Endtimes looked at Mike's data and then scanned the area. It was as he suspected.

"It's a portal. They must have gone through it. That is why you suddenly lost contact. I'm going to go down there, but I'll stay in contact with you. Hopefully, they will be back soon."

With that, *Endtimes* transported down to the base camp.

The sky was overcast, and there was evidence of recent rain. Plants growing near the stream had a yellow-green color to them with tiny deep red flowers. The stream was swiftly flowing. The mountain range opposite the mesa had a red-brown color with veins of black randomly coursing horizontally through them.

Endtimes walked through the camp looking for anything that might give him a clue. He accessed the main computer and found the same lack of info. He checked each individual dome with similar results. They hadn't been there long enough to leave any logs.

Mike called down to *Endtimes*. Some strange life signs just popped up on his scans. They were about 3220 kilometers from the camp in a forest near the planet's equator.

"They just appeared out of nowhere on the screen. Two, now five. Now seven. They are organic and large. Other than that, I can't get any more information."

"Send the coordinates to the other Ships and I'll scan here. Thanks, Mike."

Endtimes jetted to the top of the mesa and began scanning in the life signs direction. He counted eight of them. They were ten to fifteen meters tall and weighed two to five tons. They were organic, registering a large respiratory system with six lungs. A small head was perched on a long thick neck that ended in a rounded body with a long tail at the other end. They appeared to walk on four muscular legs and had a grey-green skin color. They were munching on some tree leaves. He wondered why they hadn't shown up on the initial scans of the planet. But there they were. He scanned his databases and found an 80% match with Earth's dinosaurs. He had found Harry's dinosaurs, perhaps. They were far enough away as to not be a threat to him. He sent his scanning to the Ships, attaching a priority note to Harry.

"Is *Shiva* still circumnavigating the galaxy?" *Endtimes* asked.

"Yes, she is. She is on the other side of the galaxy right now."

"Ask her to head here and give her all the info we have. I'm thinking she could send down her avatar to investigate those creatures."

"Done. She's headed this way," Mike responded.

"I'll stay down here on this side. If there is no communication in an hour, Mike, find the *Vera Rubin* and ask her to come here."

"Will do. Last I heard, she was in this sector helping some organics who were nearly wiped out by an earthquake. There were two other ships with her so, hopefully, she can break off and come here," Mike replied.

Endtimes went back to the campsite and entered the cave. He scanned every millimeter, looking for clues, then came upon the portal and scanned it. He sat down on a rock and stared at it, trying to will it to give up its secrets. His scans showed that the force field was an EM signature not of this universe. He thought the portal must be a conduit to another universe. He knew the LGM originally came from another one.

As he sat, he thought about what had happened so far. He focused on the force, or wind, that blew them away. It wasn't natural. It had signatures of artificial energy readings. He had scanned for those signatures but found nothing. He hoped that whatever generated it depleted the energy. It would explain why they weren't attacked the second time.

Suddenly the colors of the portal wavered, going from the greenish yellow to a blue-green. The tinkling noise stopped, and a low hum took its place. A LGM walked through it. They startled each other. *Endtimes* had pointed his blaster at the portal while Hymir had his gun out as well. They both laughed in relief as they put their weapons away.

"*Endtimes*! So good to see you. The others are stuck on the other side; I could go through since I am originally from that universe. Details later. There should be a device on this side powering the field."

They both looked around the hole. After several minutes, they found on the right side of the portal, a signal emanating from under a large rock. *Endtimes* moved the rock so that Hymir could get to the device. He punched in a few symbols and the field shut off. The rest of the group hurried through it.

"One more hour and that black hole would have eaten us!" Harry exclaimed. "Good to see you *Endtimes* and thank you, Hymir, that was close."

"Check your EM monitors to make sure you didn't get an extra dose of the stuff," Iryna said. Everyone was okay.

The two techs were walking next to the stretcher that Oran was on. She was still weak, but was awake. The others followed. Iryna and *Torgun* had totes filled with various medicines and small instruments. Lund was carrying a small metal box filled with data files on the Porés.

As Hymir reset the portal parameters, Harry asked if this universe was in any danger from the black hole.

"I don't think so. I think I can collapse the portal by doing this." He punched a few buttons on the controller and it vanished. In its place was just a smooth rock wall several meters thick. It also showed that a device located downstream from the base camp generated the space wind. It was nearly depleted of energy.

"What about getting the M-droids to look at the generator? Perhaps they could manufacture another one. Might be a useful thing to have," I asked.

"Good idea. I'll send a message to them. The device for it shouldn't be too big to carry," Hymir replied. "*Endtimes*, have you seen any evidence of the Porés? They should read as bipedal, similar to humans."

"No, but we have found some other life forms. I asked *Shiva* if she could investigate them. I just sent a message to the *Vera Rubin* to head here. She was in the sector. She will be interested in Oran's wound and the medicine that healed her," *Endtimes* said.

"I wasn't sure if it would work, but it did. Pelu ran some tests and found that the medicine may cause an upset stomach as a side effect," Hymir replied. "There were no serious side effects that we could see. They made the medicine from plants on the planet. If we want more, we'll have to make it ourselves."

"That shouldn't be a problem," Harry replied.

CHAPTER 9
TIME IS UNREDEEMABLE

C hapter 9

THE *VERA RUBIN* signaled they were orbiting the planet and ready to receive Oran. We transported Oran, and Hymir sent all the medicines with her.

Shiva gave an initial report on the planet's life-forms. They seemed to have some kind of blocking mechanism as they popped on and off on their scanners. As *Shiva* got closer, the forms stayed registered on her scans. They would fade but then read stronger. She tried to communicate with them but got no response.

I suggested scanning the moons, starting with the larger one. It had a thin atmosphere and an underground source for water. A small encampment came into view as the moon rotated. There were several domed enclosures connected by covered walkways. Hymir sent a message to them; the response was immediate. They were the Porés who left their universe.

Harry and Hymir transported to the moon encampment. Their leader, Do'tunec remembered Hymir. The Porés had developed an alternate way to get to our universe, the portals. They discussed the closing of the portal. Do'tunec said he would make sure it was closed permanently.

Harry explained that there would be a larger expedition returning to the planet. The Porés suggested they would help after they had assurances they could stay on the moon. They had just settled into a routine, making a home for themselves and didn't want to relocate.

The Porés had little information on the lifeforms. Not wanting to disturb them and not knowing if they were hostile, they looked elsewhere for a settlement. They didn't have to look far, for the moon would suffice. They brought over habitation domes and other survival equipment, along with stores of food.

"It was the same with us. They would appear, then disappear on our long-range scanners. As we got closer to them, they would stay on the screens. They started moving towards us. We sent out standard greetings but no answer. They just slowly lumbered towards us. They are huge! We thought it was best to leave the planet."

"As best as we can tell, this area of space is devoid of intelligent life. It could be we just haven't hit on a way to communicate with the mystery beings. Is there anything you need now?" Harry asked.

"We could use a refigure unit if that is possible? I can reprogram it for Poré food. We have a small transport, perhaps, some extra fuel for it? It uses ion energy."

"Done. We may send some engineers and energy specialists to talk to you about your unique defensive machine. Oh, we also got some files left in the city close to the portal. We can transfer them to you."

"Those files sound great. I think we got all our important files, but you never know. I am so very glad to know we have found some friends. Hymir told me about the M-droids. I look forward to meeting them," Do'tunec said.

With that, we transported back to the *Houdini* and winked back to Alpha. *Vera Rubin* followed suit, informing the Ca'Keenies' homeworld of Oran's injury. A Ca'Keenie doctor met them on Alpha and transported her back for recuperation.

Harry gave Deatine his report on the recent events. She agreed to send a bigger expedition to the planet they nick-named 'Mystery.' They began preparations for it. The group gathered up more supplies and people. Iryna wanted an expert on black holes, another exobiologist and geologist. Hymir asked to return with another LGM to help with the plant life on the planet. There was also a first-contact specialist joining them. They would attempt communica-tion with the strange dinosaur-like beings on the planet. One of the Alpha ministers suggested leaving well enough alone with the planet and its inhabitants. Iryna pointed out that they needed to study the portal further, making sure it had no impact on this universe and to assist the Porés. They would do everything possible to avoid disturbing the beings.

C and Clee were reunited with Iryna. *Dogon* had trans-ported them to Alpha, where a joyful reunion ensued. There was a family discussion about returning to the planet. The three would go, but would only stay for two weeks. Iryna would lead the group, planning different projects for the fieldwork. C, along with two M-droids, would talk with the Porés about all things related to energy. They would also provide whatever extra help they might need. Clee would help her mom set up the biology lab. Hymir and Bymir would set up the botany lab. They also would liaise with the Porés. Things progressed smoothly; they left ten days later. *Endtimes* and *Vera Rubin* transported the expedition back to Mystery. *Vera Rubin* would stay within one wink jump and *Endtimes* would orbit the planet for the duration of the research. *Torgun* decided he had enough adventure for a while. He also wanted to double check his systems since the wind encounter.

We left the next day and winked to Earth. Harry did his usual flybys of the planets. I had wanted to visit the Gigs and the M-droids, but it could wait. I was eager to get back to Earth. Word was out that Hymir was the expert on any plant in the galaxy. A bit of exaggeration but I think quite deserved. Four RA planets put in requests for trees and Hymir was having them shipped from Venus 5.

Two weeks later, C and his family returned to Earth. Ian caught a ride with *Dogon* as she was headed back to Earth after giving an update on the solar system. Ian hadn't seen C and his family in a while and wanted to visit them. His jazz night club was successful. Lots of people showed up most nights. Harry and I had enjoyed a night of jazz with him.

Harry and I stayed in France. Iryna and C camped at the Gulf Coast house. And Ian was staying with them. Everyone was glad to see each other. Clee was studying to be an exobiologist like her mom. She had a focus on Earth. C and Pi continued their energy research. It surprised Harry that Pi was still in the Milky Way. Pi replied that M110 was surviving without him as he and C were trying to harness dark energy as a source.

The droids had restored parts of Paris. The buildings

and streets looked remarkably like I remembered them. Notre Dame's bells rang on the hour. We stayed in a flat in the Latin Quarter, a place I had fond memories of. I walked to the Luxembourg Gardens and saw Hymir's handiwork. It was strange not seeing the Eiffel Tower. Harry had offered to have it rebuilt, but I still refused.

The next evening, we all gathered at the Gulf Coast house. Pi and C summarized their work with dark matter. They especially welcomed it for winking. The only limit was that the Ships couldn't wink as far, but the wait time to wink again was about a millisecond.

The droids developed engines that had fuel cells that could be replaced when they were exhausted. In theory, the Ships could go for centuries with enough replacement cells. Harry had the cells added so that he didn't have to worry about locating deposits of dark matter, even though it was fairly common. C said the engines would wear out long before the cells were depleted with continuous use. Ships would manufacture the engines themselves once they got the specifications. They would retrofit ships of the Regional Alliance with the engines. They dispatched several groups of droids across RA. It all sounded good to me.

Iryna reported things were stable with the flora and fauna of Earth. The droids were an important part of that. She received weekly reports from them from around the globe. It was rare that they had any serious problems. The question was whether to have a "weather" dome for the planet. I initially thought to keep the Earth as natural as possible, but there were two recent storms that resulted in the death of several animals and some destroyed coastal habitats. I changed my mind, and the *Harry Houdini* installed the weather dome. It would monitor the global weather, and when there was a concern, it would activate.

Iryna and the droids were setting up conditions for this. I asked whether it was possible to have only parts of the planet covered since most weather was not global in scope. Snowstorms in Siberia shouldn't cause any extreme weather in the Amazon rainforest. Of course, my comment set off a discussion about butterfly and chaos theory. I left them to it.

Clee often went with her mom to help with various projects. One that held her interest was the interactions of various marine mammals. She was interested in the orcas and, with Tilly's help, studied the various orca cultures. Whales were also on her list and eventually she could go by herself with the droids to study them. The androids tutored her in mathematics and cosmology. I kept her love of art alive with occasional impromptu lessons.

WE HAD JUST RECEIVED some news via Harry's tachyon relay from the Regional Alliance. Seems like RA was voting to change the name to the Galactic Alliance. While the Earth was still an outlier, more systems near it were applying for membership. Alpha Centauri and Wolf 1061 recently joined. It was getting crowded in Earth's neck of the woods.

I thought this would be good for Earth's protection as it would mean a more consistent presence of the Ships. The M-droids have made several upgrades to the defensive domes for the planets. Several of the space stations and outposts have had similar upgrades. Discussion, however, was about Ian.

"I'm surprised he elected to become a full droid," I said. "That explains those messages I had gotten from him asking me about how I felt about having an android body. I suspected there was more to it, but I was thinking of Reedmer, not him."

"Well, he messaged me twice about the transformation process. He asked me not to tell you," Harry said.

"Oh, for goodness' sake!" I said, "that was those mysterious communiques you got from him about two to three years ago?"

"Yes, you know Ian. Privacy and all that. He was worried that if it didn't work out and he died, you would somehow blame yourself. Truth is, his organic self was failing and there wasn't anything we could do except what we did. *Dogon* did the actual transfer. She was upset that she couldn't help you more when you took that fall and crushed most of your body. I sent over all the files I had on transferring. It's not something the Ships want to delve into given our history with Andromeda organics. But I don't have a problem with it as long as it is done in extreme circumstances. Most Ships agree with this except, of course, the original Ten. And not all of them are so closed-minded."

"Like Nine and his robot impersonation. Yeah, I guess they want Reedmer to stay in his little box."

Harry smiled. "Yes, well, there's talk about giving Reedmer more freedom."

"Really, how exciting! He'd be in the ordinary world again. Wow! So, is it a done deal?" I asked. "He had asked me about the process, what it felt like and all that when I first went through with it."

"Pretty much. He'll be transferred to *Dogon,* and she'll do the procedure. *Caddis* was reluctant. He has grown fond of Reedmer and would be upset if anything went wrong. It's tricky putting an organic mind map into the Quozanant body. *Caddis* is doing some remodeling to accommodate him. It sounds like they'll use Quozanant as a home base," Harry said.

BACK IN PARIS, we walked around the Latin Quarter and sat in Luxembourg Gardens. I closed off my thoughts to Harry. I wanted to toss around ideas and feelings as I decided what I wanted to do. We would travel throughout the galaxy and beyond. I no longer felt like I had to keep tabs on Earth. Iryna had agreed to oversee Earth. She would have the droids to help. C would continue his research into exotic energy. And Clee had the solar system to play and learn in. Harry has never pushed me in any direction. He lets me make my own decisions. It was time I fully embraced my avatar self.

I opened my thoughts to Harry. He came and stood next to me, and asked if, I was sure. I nodded. He put an arm around me and kissed my cheek. We stood on the tiny balcony watching the sunset over the city. I put my head on his chest and heard that familiar heartbeat.

Here, now, I am Claire Mackenzie. I am a human being inside an avatar body. I do not age and can self-repair most injuries. I have super-human senses and strength. I can connect to vast quantities of information. I have people here who love and care about me. I am going to be around for a long, long time. Look at me, mom, dad, my head is in the clouds and I am okay.

I am at peace.

ABOUT THE AUTHOR

Brief Biography

Jan was born and raised in New Orleans. Besides red beans and rice, she was fed on a steady diet of science fiction. As an avid reader, she always wanted to write, to tell stories, but life got in the way. Finally, much later in her life, she did so. She is a painter by training with an MFA in Fine Arts from the University of New Orleans.